AS THE SPARKS FLY UPWARD

AS THE
SPARKS FLY UPWARD

GLORIA DANK

A PERFECT CRIME BOOK

DOUBLEDAY

NEW YORK LONDON TORONTO
SYDNEY AUCKLAND

A Perfect Crime Book

PUBLISHED BY DOUBLEDAY
a division of Bantam Doubleday Dell
Publishing Group, Inc.

DOUBLEDAY is a trademark of Doubleday,
a division of Bantam Doubleday Dell
Publishing Group, Inc.

Grateful acknowledgment is made for permission to reprint excerpts
from "The Love Song of J. Alfred Prufrock" in *Collected Poems, 1909–
1962* by T. S. Eliot, copyright 1936 by Harcourt Brace Jovanovich, Inc.
and copyright © 1964, 1963 by T. S. Eliot, reprinted by permission of
Harcourt Brace Jovanovich, Inc. and Faber and Faber Limited.

Book design by Patrice Fodero

Library of Congress Cataloging-in-Publication Data

Dank, Gloria.
    As the sparks fly upward / by Gloria Dank.
        p.   cm.
    "A Perfect Crime book"—T.p. verso
    I. Title.
PS3554.A5684A7   1992
813'.54—dc20   91-27800
                                                                      CIP

ISBN 0-385-42236-9
Printed in the United States of America
April 1992
FIRST EDITION

1

The phone rang at two in the morning.

Bernard, a stolid slumbering mass, did not move. Maya rolled over and sleepily picked up the phone.

"Hello?"

"Hello, Maya."

"Snooky?"

"Yes."

"Go to hell."

Maya hung up the phone with a *click*. She nestled up to her husband and instantly fell asleep.

The phone rang again.

"Hello?"

"We were disconnected," her younger brother said cheerfully. His voice sounded far away and tinny, like an early gramophone recording. "This is a terrible connection. I guess they don't have real phones up here in the woods. Still, I guess I shouldn't complain. I'm lucky to have a phone at all."

"Snooky?"

"Yes?"

1

"Where are you?"

"I'm in Vermont. A little town called Lyle."

"That's nice. And why are you calling me now?"

"Now?"

"Snooky, don't you know what time it is?"

"No," her brother said. He sounded, maddeningly, more cheerful than ever. "Is it late? My watch stopped and I don't have a clock in the cabin."

"It's two in the morning."

"Oh."

There was a pause while Snooky digested this. "Oh, well. You're awake now, aren't you? So here's my plan. You and Bernard pack your bags tomorrow and come up here for a couple of weeks. I've rented this beautiful cabin in the woods, and it's more idyllic than you can imagine. I was just out looking at the moon. It's big and yellow tonight, like Gruyère cheese. It takes up half the sky. I feel that I've never really looked at the moon before, Maya. I want you and Bernard to come up here and see it."

"Sounds nice." Maya propped up her pillow and leaned against it drowsily. "Sounds nice. I'll think about it."

"You do that. I'll expect you tomorrow night. I'll have dinner ready and waiting."

"Forget it, Snooks. We can't come that soon. I've got an article due and Bernard is working on his new book."

"Which one is this?"

"It's another one about Mrs. Woolly. He hasn't told me the plot yet."

"Well, tell Bernard he can bring his typewriter and work up here. I have the guest room all ready for you. And it's cider season, Maya, do you hear me? Cider season. There are twenty jugs of fresh cider out back."

"Sounds tempting."

"It's delicious. There's nothing like life in the wilderness, Maya. I'm happier than I've ever been."

"That would be pretty happy," said Maya. Her brother was normally a rather cheerful person.

"Yes."

"Thank you for calling, Snooks. I'm going back to sleep now. Try not to call again before morning."

"Good night, Maya. I won't call. I'm going outside to gaze at the moon."

In the morning, Bernard looked over his coffee cup, a two-handled French affair that was as big as a soup bowl, and said curtly, "No way."

Maya smiled at him. In any given situation, her husband could be counted on to deliver the misanthropic response.

"Come on, Bernard. It sounded very nice, the way Snooky described it. And we were thinking of getting away for a while, just the two of us."

"Exactly. Just the two of us."

"Snooky's no trouble."

"Don't be absurd, Maya. Snooky's nothing but trouble. He never has been and he never will be anything else."

"You could bring your typewriter and work up there just as well as you do here."

"No, I could not."

"And why is that?"

"Because I am comfortable here. I have my study and my routine and my coffee just the way I like it. It would take me a week at least to get used to being somewhere else. And also, now that we're discussing it, I don't like the idea of this cabin in the woods."

"Why not?"

"It sounds creepy." Bernard put down his cup, which clattered loudly on its saucer.

Maya regarded him fondly. Bernard Woodruff was one of the biggest men she had ever met. He was not so much large or fat as simply massive. He looked like a big good-natured bear, except that he was not good-natured. He had dark curly hair and a bristling beard and deceptively soft, twinkly brown eyes. Now he scowled at her. "I refuse to go."

"There's nothing to be afraid of. It's only Snooky."

"Snooky and a gang of psychopathic murderers roaming the woods, looking for some throats to cut." Bernard picked up the paper. "No, thank you."

"Yours is not exactly the spirit of adventure, sweetheart."

He shrugged.

The phone rang. Maya picked it up and said, "Hello?" It was her younger brother again, his voice high-pitched and tinny, as if emanating through a time warp from his childhood.

"I'm expecting you. Are you on the road yet, heading up here?"

"Not yet, Snooky."

"Why not? What's wrong? It's Bernard, isn't it? He doesn't want to come visit me, right? He says he can't work up here and he'd rather stay in Connecticut, right?"

"That's right, Snooks."

"Put him on the phone."

"He's not in a very good mood."

"Bernard never is in a good mood. Put him on."

Bernard picked up the phone impassively. "Yes?"

An absorbed expression stole over his face. "Yes . . . Yes . . . That's true . . . That's very true . . . Uh-huh . . . Yes . . . Yes, I see your point . . . That's certainly true . . . Yes . . . All right. Fine. Say the day after tomorrow. How long a drive is it? . . . And we have to bring the dog, remember. We don't go anywhere without Misty."

Misty, a small red furball at Bernard's feet, thumped her tail at the mention of her name.

"All right. I hadn't thought of it that way . . . Okay. Day after tomorrow, then. Good-bye." Bernard replaced the phone gingerly on its receiver.

Maya stared at him in astonishment. "Good Lord. What did he say?"

"He pointed out that if we visit him, we'll be staying in his place and eating his food and bothering him, instead of the other way around. It was such a novel idea that I accepted. I wouldn't mind eating Snooky's food for once."

Maya smiled. In the four years since Snooky had graduated from college, he had visited them often, showing up unexpectedly at their door and overstaying his welcome by several months.

"Good. I'll go pack," she said, rising from the table.

"I think the dog's throwing up," Bernard said.

They were on I-91 heading north for Vermont. They had just passed the Connecticut-Massachusetts border. Maya glanced into the back seat.

"Oh, God. Don't look back. It's disgusting."

"This is a new car," Bernard said mournfully.

"It is not new. It's three years old."

"Practically new."

"What do you want me to do about it, Bernard? Climb over the seat and clean it up while you're doing sixty-five miles an hour on the highway?"

"No. I'll tell you what. Let's just forget about it."

"Good idea."

"Let's ignore it, and maybe it will go away."

"Fine."

Misty retched again, miserably. Bernard stared moodily out at the unending highway.

"This was a mistake," he said. "I can feel it. Misty can feel it. Anything to do with your little brother is trouble. He's the original—what's that quote?—the original man born unto trouble, or something."

" 'Man is born unto trouble, as the sparks fly upward,' " quoted Maya. "The Book of Job."

"Exactly."

"Snooky isn't so bad, Bernard. You've never given him a chance."

"I've given him plenty of chances."

"You have not."

"Have too."

They lapsed into sullen silence. Bernard thrummed his fingers on the steering wheel. "He practically lives in my house, doesn't he?"

5

"I'll say this for you, sweetheart, you've been very forebearing. You've never turned him away."

"He's my brother-in-law."

"He'd like to be closer to you, you know. I know he would. He often talks to me about it. He'd like it if the two of you were friends."

Bernard turned his face away. In the back seat, Misty threw up.

Maya sighed and dug into the picnic hamper she had brought along. It was always like this. Her husband didn't dislike Snooky any more than he disliked anyone else, but he didn't like him any better, either. Of course, Bernard hated everyone. It was part of his charm. To be included inside the pinprick circle of his affection and concern always made her feel smug, somehow. Bernard never spoke to anyone else if he could help it, although he had to speak to Snooky sometimes, when Snooky was staying in their house. Since graduating from college, Snooky had spent his time and money wandering across the country, staying here and there as the whim suited him. He did not work; their parents, who had died years ago, had left Snooky, Maya, and their older brother, William, a large enough fortune that he did not have to work. This fact drove William nearly insane.

"I hate him," he would say. "I hate him, Maya. Do you hear me? There's nothing I hate more than him. I—I *despise* him."

William, a hardworking corporate lawyer who had raised his younger siblings after their parents died, found the mere spectacle of Snooky irritating.

"I hate the way he sits around all day," he would say in an ominous whisper to Maya. "I hate the way he lies on the couch and watches TV. He's a child of our age, Maya—a child of our age. A videohead."

His frequent lectures to Snooky on this subject, however, left William more baffled than not.

"I *do* work, William," his younger brother would say in tones of reproach. "I work in unseen ways. I hold up my end of the universe. I fulfill a useful function."

"And what is that?" William would ask, grinding his teeth.

"I umbellate, William. I umbellate."

And by the time William had rushed to the dictionary, to discover that "umbellate" had something to do with the shape in which carrots grow, and nothing to do with any kind of useful work whatsoever, Snooky would have made good his escape.

Bernard sighed deeply and turned the radio on. "How's Misty doing?"

"Better. She seems to have settled down."

"You were thinking about William, weren't you?"

"Yes. How could you tell?"

"Every time you think about him, a little involuntary spasm crosses your face. It's sort of touching."

Maya smiled and settled back in her seat.

Hours later, Bernard said gloomily, "We've missed the exit, haven't we?"

"I don't know. I don't think so."

"I'm sure we have. I think that was it, about three miles back."

"Snooky didn't give very good directions."

"Snooky never gives good directions. He's probably not even up here. He probably called from California to send us here for a laugh."

"Shut up and let me think," Maya said with some asperity. She smoothed the map on her lap and regarded it thoughtfully. Perhaps Bernard was right. It *did* seem that they had come too far . . .

"Are these the Green Mountains?"

Bernard scanned the sere, blasted winter landscape doubtfully. "I don't know. I've never been this far north before."

"We've passed Brattleboro, haven't we?"

"I think so. About five hours ago. Do you think we're in Canada yet?"

"Don't panic." Maya ran her finger along the thick green line of I-91. "At least we know what road we're on. We can always turn around and get back home if we want to. Have you seen any signs for Lebanon?"

"No."

"Maybe we should stop for directions."

"All right. I'll get off at the next exit."

They got off of the highway and consulted with a small, wizened man at a Mobil gas station. There was much gesticulating and gesturing. Their guide pointed north, then west. Apparently they were still far from their destination. Bernard stood shivering in the freezing cold air, listening patiently for several minutes, at the end of which time the old man shook his hand in fond farewell and disappeared into his heated booth. Bernard got back into the car.

"We're doomed," he said.

"That bad?"

"Doomed," said Bernard, breathing heavily through his nose. "We're still far away, dark is coming on, and I have already begun to forget everything that man just told me."

"Repeat it to me right away."

Bernard repeated it.

"All right," said Maya, grabbing the map. "I see where we are. Let's go."

They headed north, crawling with what seemed like painful slowness along the thick green map line of I-91. At last Maya cried out, "There's our exit!" and they left the highway and drove for a long time along a small two-lane road. The area was mountainous and wooded and very beautiful, but the two travelers were not in the mood to appreciate natural beauty. Bernard ate his way steadily through the contents of the picnic hamper ("Knowing Snooky, he won't have dinner ready—or worse, he'll have expected *us* to bring it"), and Misty whimpered softly in the growing darkness.

At last a few lights glowed ahead, and they found themselves on a small main street encircling a village green.

"This must be Lyle," said Maya, switching on the reading lamp in the car ceiling. "Go straight. Snooky's cabin is outside the village. Go straight until the road forks, then take the far right-hand turn. He said it's a little rocky, so be careful."

They drove through the village, passing houses with lights shining from their windows, seeming (Bernard thought miserably) very warm and civilized and comforting. He imagined everyone in Lyle sitting down to a hot dinner. After about ten minutes the road forked, and Bernard slowed to a halt. He turned on his brights and peered dubiously at the small dirt road to the right.

"There?"

"Yes."

"Are you sure?"

"Yes."

"Your brother lives up there?"

"Yes."

"Up that little dirt path?"

"Yes."

Bernard made the turn with difficulty. The road meandered through a thick forest. All was strangely silent and ghostly. The car headlights careened violently between the trees as Bernard cursed and bumped over the rocky path. Finally Maya said with relief, *"There."*

Bernard forced the unwilling car up the final stretch (Misty, in the back seat, had given up her spirit by this time and lay with her tongue lolling out, drooling miserably), and Snooky's cabin came into sight. It stood in a small clearing among the trees. It was brightly lit from within and looked large and comfortable. There was a white picket fence surrounding it, with a little yard. Bernard came to a halt next to a small red Honda that was parked by the fence.

"Not bad," he said, peering through the window at the cabin. "You're sure this is it? That's your brother's car?"

"His rented car. You know Snooky doesn't own anything. He's like a monk—no possessions."

"What do you think—is Misty still alive?"

"You get the luggage out, and I'll deal with Misty. Here comes Snooky."

9

"Welcome to the wilderness!" cried her brother, bounding down the front steps.

"Go to hell," Bernard greeted him.

"Bernard, so good to see you. And you, Maya. Miserable trip? That's what I thought. Bernard hates to travel, I know that. How about the dog? Still with us? Good. Let me help you with the luggage. I hate to tell you this, Maya, but the back seat is not as clean as I presume it was when Misty got into it."

"Don't talk about it, Snooks. We'll think about it in the morning. Did you prepare supper?"

"Supper? I thought you were bringing supper? Just kidding," he said at the sight of Bernard's stricken face. "I have everything all ready. Come on in and get warm."

He led the way indoors. There was a spacious living room, with a fire burning in the hearth and two comfortable-looking sofas. Part of the living room was taken up by a long wooden table which was set for three people, complete with place mats, stoneware dishes, and polished silverware. Crystal goblets glittered in the firelight, and Snooky had uncorked a bottle of red wine that stood in the center of the table, reflecting a dull crimson from its depths. The kitchen was small but modern, and two bedrooms led off from the main room, both with antique bedsteads and plump quilts piled high on thick mattresses. All was crisp, fresh and clean, and a heavenly scent drifted through the air.

"Dinner," Snooky said, putting their luggage into one of the bedrooms. "I went all out. I knew Bernard would need something to console him after the trip."

Maya picked up one of the crystal goblets and toyed with it absently. "I can see you've been roughing it."

"None of it's mine, of course. It belongs to the people I rented this place from. I have it for a couple of months, then they're coming back from France and they'll want to spend weekends here over the winter. Good skiing in this area. They have good taste, don't they? Not bad for a weekend retreat. Have you seen the Cuisinart in the kitchen yet? All the most modern amenities."

"So what's all this babbling about life in the wilderness?"

"I can't explain it, Maya. You have to live here a while and get a sense for it. It's so *different* from the city." Snooky sat down on one of the sofas and stretched out his long legs. "You have to be here and smell the air and get a feel for how things work. It's like your whole metabolism slows down and relaxes. You'll see. It's wonderful. I'm never living in a city again."

Bernard came out of the guest bedroom. "Misty's getting her sea legs back," he announced. "When's dinner?"

"It's almost ready, Bernard. Sit down by the fire and enjoy yourself. I made your favorite: beef stew."

Bernard's grim expression did not change. He sat down and stretched out his hands to the cheerful flames. "I take it there's no central heating?"

"This is the wilderness, Bernard. Rural living. Life in the wild. Of course there's no central heating. I take logs from the woodpile out back and I put them in the fireplace and I light a fire with them and then they burn. That's how people stayed warm for thousands of years."

"Primitive."

"But effective. You have to admit it, don't you? This cabin is a lot better than you thought it'd be."

Bernard grunted.

Snooky turned to his sister and smiled. In the firelight, Bernard noted dourly how similar their faces were. Snooky was five years younger, which put him in his mid-twenties, but they had the same lean, elongated frame and the same intelligent, angular face. Maya had her light brown hair cut in a severe pageboy, and Snooky wore his combed back casually from his forehead, but there was no mistaking them for anything but sister and brother. Bernard sighed and hunkered forward toward the flames. With his massive bearlike build, he sometimes felt as if he had been raised on another planet.

"Is there electricity?" asked Maya.

Snooky looked pained. "Yes, there is electricity. This is

11

the wilderness, Maya. It's not Guyana. There's a light switch on the wall behind you."

"Does the bathroom work?" asked Bernard.

"Yes, the bathroom works. There is hot and cold running water. This is Vermont, Bernard, not Mars. I think the stew is ready. Come to the table."

The dinner (as most of Snooky's meals were when he put his mind to it) was excellent. Even Bernard could find no fault. The beef stew was thick and meaty, filled with potatoes and carrots and onions and green peppers, swimming in a rich garlicky sauce. There was fresh-baked whole wheat bread ("Don't look at me," said Snooky. "I bought it in the village"), homemade apple sauce ("From fresh-picked apples, courtesy of the Cuisinart"), stewed pumpkin with cinnamon and raisins ("It's nothing, I made it myself—delicious, isn't it?"), and red wine. Snooky and Maya chatted, catching up on the past few months since they had seen each other. Bernard did not join in their conversation; they did not expect him to. He devoted himself to the food and ate his way steadily through every course offered to him. For dessert, Snooky brought out a huge cherry pie with mocha nut ice cream. Bernard's eyes gleamed in the candlelight. Afterward, Snooky produced steaming mugs of apple cider with nutmeg and cloves, and they relaxed around the fire. Misty, having crept out from the bedroom to seek warmth by the hearth, had recovered enough to eat some of the food they had brought along for her. Now she lay collapsed, a pile of tangled red hair, at Bernard's feet.

"Tomorrow we'll get up early and go for a walk in the woods," announced Snooky.

"No, thank you," said Bernard.

"Why not?"

"I'm not getting up early."

"Whenever. The peak of the foliage is past, of course, but it's still very beautiful in its own way. I've become a day person, Maya. Can you believe that? I get up early and go roaming in the woods. You haven't smelled anything until you've smelled the mist rising off those big golden fungus things at the base of the trees." He glanced at Bernard with a faint smile on his lips. "You're not much of a naturalist, are you, Bernard?"

"I don't care what you go out and snuffle early in the mornings, Snooky. I don't care what you do. Just as long as you don't put those big golden fungus things, as you put it so elegantly, into the stew, I could really care less."

"Bernard hates the city," remarked Maya with affection, "but he also hates the woods."

"Bernard hates everywhere except for his own house."

"Bernard," said Bernard sternly, "doesn't like to be referred to in the third person, as if he weren't there."

There was a contented silence, broken only by the hissings and poppings and cracklings of the flames. Misty yawned thunderously. They sprawled on the sofas, lulled into a happy stupor by the gentle heat.

"Have you met any of the people who live in that town we passed through?" asked Maya at last, stifling a yawn.

"Who, me?" said Snooky, roused from his contemplation of the fire. "Oh, yes. You know me, Maya. I can't go anywhere without meeting a few people. I've made some friends."

Maya smiled at him. Snooky was not much in the way of working, but friendship was something he had a preternatural gift for. He could not go anywhere, in his extensive wanderings, without meeting people and striking up an acquaintance. It was something else William hated about him: William, who had no friends, just business partners.

"Anyone special?" she asked now.

"One. Her name is Sarah. You'll meet her tomorrow. She has an interesting family. They've invited us over for lunch. We'll go there when we get back from our walk."

"Don't make too many dates for us, Snooky. You know how Bernard feels about that. And we did come up here to work."

"Yes. What's the name of the newest book, Bernard?"

Bernard, who made a living writing children's books, did not reply.

"Sheep or rats?"

Bernard stared stonily into the fireplace.

"*Mrs. Woolly Meets the Snowplow*? *Mr. Whiskers Sings Mozart*?"

No reply.

"Don't be angry with me, Bernard. I'm only asking. I'm just expressing some interest in your career, you know that."

"He doesn't like you taking an interest in his career, Snooky," said Maya sharply. "You know better than to ask questions. It's not easy for him to get started. He's having a little difficulty with this one."

"It's going to be about Mrs. Woolly," said Bernard.

"Ah!"

"She takes a trip somewhere, I don't know where. Somewhere exotic, like Baghdad or Burma. She gives advice. You know how it is."

Snooky nodded. He was familiar with Mrs. Woolly, a kind-eyed ewe who peered mistily and nearsightedly through her spectacles and dispensed well-meant advice like candy. "How about you, Maya? How are the articles going?"

Maya, who wrote for a small, local magazine entitled *The Animal World*, shrugged and said, "Okay. I'm working on an article about the pronghorn antelope. That reminds me. You haven't seen any deer around here, have you?"

"There are no deer around here, Maya. Just hunters. I see them every day, in the woods. They creep along, trying not to shoot each other. Extremely annoying. By the way, Bernard, it's small animal season up here. If I were you, I wouldn't let Misty run loose in the woods. She might be mistaken for something. All those people seem to live for is a small moving target."

"All right. Any bears?" said Bernard.

"Bears? I haven't seen any. Why do you ask?"

"Just wondering."

There was a silence.

"Any mountain lions?"

1 4

"Mountain lions? I think you have the wrong area of the country entirely, Bernard."

"Any murderers or psychopaths loose in the woods?"

"Not too many. Just the usual, you know, that run happy and free all the time."

"Anything dangerous at all?"

"To tell you the truth, the most frightening thing I've encountered so far was a bug that got into my bedroom and sat on my bedstead looking at me. The largest thing I've ever seen, all legs and wings and about a hundred pairs of eyes. Horrible. Really horrible. It took some doing to get it out of the cabin, I'll tell you."

Maya and Bernard stifled yawns. Misty was already fast asleep.

"Well, I can only pray for the sake of your sanity that it doesn't visit you one night. I nearly packed my bags and left for New York City."

A little while later Snooky, yawning, said, "Time for bed," and showed them with a flourish into the guest room. He left them with repeated admonitions to get up early the next morning. The room was freezing cold, but Bernard discovered with joy that it was toasty warm under the goosedown quilt. He kissed his wife a sleepy good-night and rolled over on his side. Misty, left abandoned by the hearth, crept trembling into their room, her toenails clicking on the wooden floor. She sat and whined until Bernard lifted her onto the quilt, where she snuggled in happily between them. Soon all three of them were sound asleep, although (as Maya had often remarked testily to Bernard) only the dog snored.

The next morning Bernard and Maya awoke to the heavenly smell of fresh coffee wafting through the cabin. Maya got out of bed, shivering in her pink flannel nightgown. She went to the window and pushed aside the green gingham curtains. It was a bright sunlit day; the sky was a perfect translucent blue. The road leading up to the cabin, which had seemed so dark and threatening the night before, now appeared to curve away gently through the trees. The forest, which last night had leaned in menacingly around them, tall shapes looming through the darkness, now looked sylvan and welcoming with the sunlight slanting through the bare branches. She sniffed the air. "I smell bacon."

"And coffee," said Bernard, throwing back the covers.

"And eggs."

"And toast."

"*Breakfast!*" cried Snooky, appearing like a vision in his ratty blue bathrobe at their door. "Nippy, isn't it? I've started the fire. You two sleep much too late. It's nearly eight o'clock. I've been up for hours."

"Stop bragging," said Maya. "It isn't becoming."

"Go take showers or whatever. I'll have breakfast ready when you get out." He vanished with a wave of a spatula.

"It's amazing," Maya said to her husband in a whisper. "I never thought Snooky would take to the wilderness this way."

"I never thought Snooky could survive more than fifty feet away from a TV," said Bernard. "He used to hang onto our remote control like a life raft, if I remember correctly."

After breakfast, which consisted of perfect scrambled eggs, bacon, coffee, toast, raspberry jam, and hot buttery croissants, as well as (for Bernard only) a thick slice of the cherry pie left over from the evening before, Snooky said, "Now for a walk in the woods. I insist you go out and smell the fungus, both of you. My day will not be complete otherwise."

Maya was interested in smelling the fungus ("Maybe I could get an article out of it"), but Bernard refused point-blank.

"Forget it," he said, sitting down on one of the sofas and stretching out his hands toward the fire. "I have to get some work done."

There was much cajoling and whining on Snooky's part, but Bernard held firm. It was decided that only Snooky and Maya would go.

"Of course we'll take Misty," said Snooky, reaching

down to pat the fluffy red back. "You don't mind going, do you, Misty? You're not a stick-in-the-mud like Bernard. You have a sense of adventure. You know, Maya, maybe we should put a bell on her or something. I'd never forgive myself if somebody took a shot at her."

"I'm not putting a bell on her," said Bernard sourly. "And what if somebody takes a shot at either of you?"

Snooky shook his head. "They seem to be able to tell human beings from mice or rabbits or whatever it is they're trying to kill. I guess their own survival rate wouldn't be too high if they couldn't tell the difference. Misty just looks so—so woodlike, if you know what I mean."

"I'll put her leash on," suggested Maya wisely, "and keep her right by me. Good-bye, darling. Good luck with your work."

"Good-bye."

"He's not going to work," said Snooky, once they were safely out in the woods. He picked his way along a narrow dirt path that twisted and bent between the trees. "He's going to sit there for a while, and then he's going to go get another cup of coffee and the rest of that cherry pie. I know him."

Misty, trembling with excitement, strained eagerly at the leash, then stopped dead in her tracks to examine something in the bracken. "Come on, Misty. Come on," said Maya, tugging at the leash.

"Here's the fungus," said Snooky. "Give a whiff."

Maya leaned down and inhaled deeply. The faint, earthy, woodsy, brown smell wafted up from the large golden globes that were clustered at the base of an oak tree. It smelled of autumn, of moist crumbly dirt and burrowing insects and red leaves crackling underfoot. "Delicious!"

Snooky was delighted. "I knew you'd say that. Bernard will be sorry he missed this. There's a view over here."

He led her over to a place where the trees thinned out. Pine-covered mountains hung serenely in the distance, undulating against the pale blue sky. Maya was impressed. "Very nice, Snookers. That's a ski slope over there?"

Snooky squinted against the morning sunlight. "Yes. I think so. I don't know. I'm not much of a skier myself. You know how William feels about that, My. All those expensive skiing lessons in vain."

William, who was an expert skiier (he and his family spent part of every winter holiday season in Gstaad, skiing the Swiss Alps), had wasted vast amounts of money, time and emotional energy trying to teach Snooky to ski. William, who was Maya's elder by a decade, had taken her and Snooky as young children out to an easy slope in the Poconos and then proceeded to tear his hair out as he watched Snooky wobbling his way downhill. Maya had mastered the essentials fairly quickly, although she never became more than merely proficient; but the six-year-old Snooky, who was a gifted athlete in nearly every sport he tried—Snooky, who was long-limbed and coordinated and rarely moved with a wasted motion—had somehow never gotten beyond the basics, ploughing determinedly downhill with his skis pointed inward toward each other, and falling down in every snowdrift he passed. William would sweep downhill, pick him out of the snowdrift, and set him on his feet again, but to no avail. Later the personalized family lessons gave way to exorbitantly priced professional ski instruction, but with the same result. Maya knew perfectly well that Snooky was refusing to learn simply because he knew it annoyed William. William, who was no fool, knew it also, but he could not help being annoyed. They went on like this for several winter seasons, until one day William threw up his hands in despair. "I give up. Take up bowling, or jai alai, or pick-up-sticks, or what you will. I wash my hands of you. You will never ski the Swiss Alps."

Maya was startled out of her thoughts by Misty, who lunged forward suddenly and began to bark. Snooky was laughing. "It's a woodchuck. Practically the same size as Misty. She wouldn't stand a chance. I never knew she had such a bloodlust in her."

The woodchuck gave them one disdainful glance and then scuttled away through the underbrush, a small brown furry shape moving with unexpected speed. Misty stood panting and disappointed. Maya gathered up the leash and said, "Time to head back, Snookers. Bernard must be convinced we've left him alone to die in the woods."

"Bernard is making his third cup of coffee, and is perfectly happy," said Snooky, but he obediently turned around and started back along the path.

When they reached the cabin, they found Bernard hunched forward on the sofa, typing away determinedly. He had found an old wooden crate out back, near the wood pile, and had lugged it in and placed it between the sofa and the fire. He had balanced his electric typewriter on top of it, dragged over one of the floor lamps, and was working away, the very picture of concentration. On a small table at Bernard's elbow was an empty plate, smeared with the moist red innards of the cherry pie, and a steaming cup of coffee.

"Why is the typewriter on top of the unsteady crate, while the coffee cup is on the table?" asked Snooky.

"The crate is taller," said Bernard, not taking his eyes from the page.

"I could find you a better table if you want."

"Fine."

Maya gave her husband a kiss. "Everything all right? Anything happen here while we were gone?"

Bernard took a large red pencil and made an undecipherable mark on the page. "Somebody called."

"Who?"

"I don't know. I wrote it down. Over there." He motioned vaguely toward the telephone, which was on the floor. By the phone was a torn scrap of paper.

"Sarah. Lunch," read Snooky. "Thank you, Bernard. Clear and to the point. Did she say anything else?"

"She asked where you were."

"What did you tell her?"

"I told her you were out sniffing fungus in the woods. She seemed to understand."

1 9

"Sarah does understand. She's a wonderful girl. I can't wait for both of you to meet her. Let me get changed, Maya, and then we can go."

On the way over in the car, with Maya driving and Snooky directing from the back seat, he filled them in about his new girlfriend.

"She's a few years younger than me. Turn left here, Maya. She just graduated from college a year or so ago. She came home to figure out what she wants to do with her life. She lives with her aunt, who raised her from the time she was little. Her parents died, just like ours. Isn't that sad, Maya? Don't you think we have a lot in common?"

"You mean she's an orphan and she also has no job, just like you?"

"There's a difference, though. She *wants* to have a job. She's thinking about going to law school. I keep trying to dissuade her. Think of what law school does to you. I mean, look at William."

"William was that way before law school."

"Was he really? Anyway, Sarah's—well, I think she's beautiful. I don't know if you'll agree. You have funny taste sometimes. After all, you picked Bernard, didn't you?"

"Bernard is very handsome," said Bernard.

"Well, I don't know. If you like mountain men. Anyway, we just clicked right away. You know how it is. There's all sorts of trouble going on in her family right now because her aunt, who's superrich, I mean really loaded, is going out with this younger guy who's clearly after her money. Everybody keeps telling her so, but she won't listen. Sarah's sort of upset about it."

"This is fascinating," said Bernard. "I'm so glad we could hear all about your little friend."

Snooky was unperturbed. "Do you see this house here, Maya? It belongs to the Grunwald sisters. They're strange. They're like something out of a nineteenth-century English gothic novel. You know, the two elderly sisters who live together and crochet little things for the town's babies and bake bread for the vicar (what *is* a vicar, Maya? Why don't we have any in America?), and they're the first ones to see the vampire or realize the rats have been called down to overwhelm their little village. You know what I'm saying. And this house here, the blue one with the black shutters, the Victorian, that belongs to Sarah's uncle. That's her aunt's brother, not her husband. He's a weird guy. Maybe you'll meet him someday. Isn't this a charming village?"

They were driving down the main street of the little village of Lyle. Maya wended her way carefully around the town square, which boasted a red brick town hall and an enormous oak tree, leafless now in the chill November air. There were houses dotted on either side of the street, ranging from Victorian-looking monstrosities to ramshackle clapboard houses to new, neatly tended ranch houses. There seemed to be no one architectural style. People had come to Lyle and had built whatever they liked and felt comfortable with. There were a few shops along the main street— Snooky pointed out the bakery ("That's where I got the bread and the cherry pie—you'll make a note of that, won't you, Bernard?") and a hardware store. There was even a little red-brick library tucked back among a copse of trees, set away from the road.

"Turn right. Go down here. Turn left at the light. Okay. Turn at that little road there. Good. Here we are."

"You seem to know your way around," commented Maya.

"I do. I always know my way around. That's my second priority whenever I move someplace new."

"And your first is . . . ?"

"To meet as many people as possible."

"Well, you seem to have succeeded here," said Maya as they turned into a tree-lined drive. A sign on a low stone wall bordering the drive said simply, in gold letters, HUGO'S FOLLY.

"Hugo's Folly?" said Maya.

"Hugo was Sarah's aunt's late husband. He had a sense

of humor, that's all. He said if he ever made enough money to build the kind of house he wanted, he would put a gold sign out front that said Hugo's Folly. All right?"

"Looks like he made enough money," remarked Bernard dryly, as the house came into view.

"He did."

The house was Victorian in design, huge and sprawling, with wings, annexes, twisted chimneys, and turrets reaching to the sky, small lead-paned windows in the eaves and two massive stone lions guarding either side of the entryway. It was gray with dark green shutters. It stood on the top of a hill, the land falling away from it in gentle curves on either side.

"This is unbelievable," said Bernard, looking out the window.

"It's the same inside, I'm sorry to say," said Snooky. "A real period piece. Sarah's uncle said he wanted room to breathe. Well, he got it, and he filled it up with all kinds of fantastic stuff. Wait until you see."

"Looks like a ghost house," said Maya.

"Well, don't say anything to Sarah, she grew up here and she'll be offended. Bernard, on your best behavior, please. Here she is."

A slim, slight figure bounded off the front steps and came to meet them. Snooky's girlfriend had shining dark red hair reaching to her shoulders, a small delicate face, large hazel eyes, and an inquisitive expression. She had pale, freckled skin and a large, generous mouth. Her features were too haphazard to be truly beautiful, but her eyes were intelligent and her glance, when she greeted Snooky, was (Maya was glad to note) affectionate. She shook hands with Maya and Bernard, and Snooky introduced her as Sarah Tucker.

"Come meet my aunt," she said. "She's waiting inside, with a friend of hers."

"Bobby?" said Snooky.

The girl gave a slight, involuntary grimace. "I'm afraid

so. He's around all the time now. She invited him, of course. And Dwayne is here, too."

"Quite a crowd," murmured Snooky, following her up the steps.

"I hate crowds," said Bernard to Maya.

"I know you do, dear. And after this, you won't have to meet anybody new the entire time you're here. Isn't that right, Snooky?"

As Bernard entered the house, the huge wooden door swinging open before him, he had the same dizzying, mind-reeling sensation he had had once on an ill-fated trip to the Manhattan Bloomingdale's store. The inside was dark, with mirrors everywhere, reflecting the dim overhead light in garish patterns. There seemed to be too many objects crammed into one space; Bernard had a confused impression of a stone statuary in dismal shapes, heavy carpets, miniature stone lions glaring at him from either side (replicas of the ones on the front steps), and dark, angry-looking portraits crowded at random onto the walls. They passed through a small foyer into what must, Bernard reasoned, be the living room, a vast space crowded with tiny objects. There were small silver frames, clustered in companionable groups, the photographs inside (mostly black and white) looking at each other blankly, with no sign of recognition. There were floor lamps and table lamps, fringed in scarlet; there was a large blue-and-white Persian rug on the floor; the draperies were red velvet; and there seemed to be mirrors everywhere: on the walls, on the wooden cabinet in the corner. This room was flooded with light from the tall floor-to-ceiling windows. Bernard felt like squeezing his eyes shut and screaming. The room looked like someone's nightmare of nineteenth-century Victorian interior design.

"Where's the mausoleum?" he murmured to Maya.

"What?"

"Didn't the Victorians all have mausoleums out back? Didn't they have kind of a fascination with death?"

2 3

An elderly woman rose from a chair and came forward. "So pleased to meet you. I'm Irma Ditmar, Sarah's aunt. Snooky speaks about you so often; it's wonderful to get to meet you at last. This is Bobby Fuller, and this is my nephew Dwayne Costa. He and Sarah are cousins. Oh, all these family relationships, it's so confusing, isn't it? Please sit down, lunch is almost ready, isn't it, Sarah dear?"

"Yes, Aunt Irma."

Bernard reached out for a fringed chair. There were so many tiny fragile-looking objects in the room that he did not trust himself to move. He eased himself into the chair with a sigh of relief.

Sarah's aunt Irma was still chattering away. She was a tiny, bright-eyed woman with a face like a little bird. She had neatly styled curly gray hair and bright green eyes. Her face was, under the makeup she wore, plainly weather-beaten and creased. She wore an expensive green silk dress and far too much makeup. There were gold earrings in her ears and a heavy gold bracelet on her wizened hand. "Oh, yes," she was saying now to Maya, "I know the house is a monstrosity, inside and out, but it's the way Hugo liked it —my husband, you know—and even though it's been nearly fifteen years, why, I can't think of changing anything, you understand . . ."

Maya was murmuring something suitably sympathetic.

Bernard squinted around the room. The bright light and the mirrors made it difficult to open his eyes. The man who had been introduced as Bobby Fuller—the one who, Bernard did not doubt, was Irma Ditmar's "friend"—was at least thirty years younger than she. He was a few years older than Bernard, which would place him in his mid-thirties. He had pale blond hair, so pale as to be almost silver, and a narrow, aesthetic-looking face. He was dressed in a natty gray tweed outfit, something that Ralph Lauren would advertise as suitably "country," and looked as if it had taken him a long time to choose it and put it on. He gazed languidly back at Bernard. "Here for long?"

Bernard had already decided that he did not like him. "Vermont or this room?"

Bobby Fuller brushed a tiny piece of lint off his trousers with a snap of his fingers and shrugged in a slow, catlike manner. "This room."

"I hope not."

"I wouldn't worry. This room is the worst. It's dedicated to Irma's former husband and his lack of taste. The rest of the house is better."

"I hope so."

Fuller nodded. He glanced at Irma, who was still chattering away to Maya. "Sarah tells me you write children's books?" The slight inflection at the end made it a question, almost a point of disbelief.

"That's right."

Fuller gazed at him out of his pale, pale blue eyes. "You don't look to me like a children's book author."

"And what does that look like?"

"Oh, you know." He waved a languid hand expressively. "Tiny women babbling about mice, that kind of thing. Although I must say that when I was younger I was devoted to the Miss Bianca books. She could do no wrong, to me. And the Borrowers, of course. And Robin Hood. And, of course, Winnie-the-Pooh."

Bernard felt himself thawing slightly. He, too, when he was younger, had been a fan of Miss Bianca, mainly because her most devoted admirer in the books was named Bernard: the faithful, the loyal, the true Bernard.

"Lunch is served, everyone," said Sarah.

The dining room, Bernard discovered to his vast relief, looked almost normal. There were French windows with a view out over the sloping lawn and the leafless trees, and the walls were covered with a muted cream-colored silk wallpaper. The heavy draperies were a matching cream, almost an earth tone, and the Persian carpet under the long mahogany table was gold, blue, and brown. The effect was pleasing, and (Bernard felt) easy on the eyes. The portraits on the walls looked down on them in an irritated way, as if annoyed to see the room used by the living, but in this setting they did not appear quite as malignant as in the foyer. Bernard looked around for his wife but found to his distress that she was being directed to the other end of the table. He found himself seated between Sarah and Sarah's cousin Dwayne Costa. Dwayne was a handsome young man in his early twenties with blue-black hair, strong features, and a rather vacuous, mobile face. He smiled at Bernard and said, "So you're Snooky's brother-in-law."

Bernard remained silent. This was something that he liked to admit only under duress.

"Your wife is very striking-looking."

Bernard nodded. This was true, but he did not see why a total stranger would see fit to comment on it.

"Snooky's told us a lot about you," said Dwayne, flailing about for something to say.

"Really? What?"

"Oh, you know . . . your work, and stuff like that."

"I see."

"You write about sheep?"

"No," said Bernard. "I write nonfiction books about the history of nuclear power. My latest book is entitled *Peaceful Uses of Atomic Energy in a Nuclear Age.*"

"How fascinating," Dwayne said warmly. "Snooky didn't mention anything about that."

"When I'm not writing about nuclear power, I do research on eleventh-century Japanese novelists. Have you ever read *The Pillow Book of Lady Murasaki*?"

"Lady Murasaki . . . no, no, I'm afraid not."

Bernard nodded and sighed. "So few people have."

"Here's the soup," said Dwayne. "Have some?"

"Thank you."

Bernard tried the soup, a pale cream-colored liquid that mysteriously matched the draperies and wallpaper of the room. It was very good. He slurped it up happily, thinking he had discouraged further conversation; but after a pause, his companion said cheerfully, "I hope to be a writer myself."

"How fascinating."

"A poet, actually. I've had some stuff published in a Manhattan poetry review. It's so exciting to see your work in print, isn't it? I'm sure you feel that way about your books."

"Yes."

"The only problem is, it's damn hard to make a living. Did your nuclear power book sell?"

"It's in its eighth printing," said Bernard modestly.

Dwayne stared at him, his mouth open. "Eighth printing . . . why, that's wonderful! Just wonderful. I don't know if I'll ever have that kind of success. I'm living here in Lyle right now, sponging off my stepfather. He's Irma's brother. Terrible to be dependent, isn't it? But he never seems to mind. And it gives me time for my poetry. I also dabble in photography a bit—just a bit—I've had some pictures displayed locally, but nothing professional, of course . . ."

Bernard switched his mind off. While Dwayne droned on happily about his nascent careers, Bernard tuned in to the other conversations around him. In particular, he stared hard at Maya, at the other end of the long rectangular table, willing her to look his way. After a moment, she looked up. Their eyes met in a look of complete understanding. She smiled brightly at something Bobby Fuller had just said, and murmured a response. Bernard looked around the table. Snooky, he noted, was (as usual) doing three things at once, all with his usual flair. He was talking animatedly with Irma Ditmar, stuffing his face with food, and keeping an eye on everyone's reactions around the table. That was something he excelled at: being the soul of charm and amiability, and at the same time taking in what everyone around him was doing. Bernard finished his soup and reached for the bread basket. Sociability was for the Snookys of this world, he thought, smearing a large chunk of butter on a wholewheat roll.

On his left, Dwayne had finally lapsed into contented, well-fed silence. On his right, Sarah Tucker turned to him. "I hear you have a dog."

"Yes."

"Misty, right?"

"Yes. A small red animal. Looks like a mop."

"I like dogs," said Sarah. She smiled, crinkling the pale freckled skin over the bridge of her nose. "Sometimes I think I like dogs better than people."

Bernard looked at her thoughtfully. This was a sentiment with which he could thoroughly agree.

"I suppose a lot of people feel that way," she was saying.

"Not really."

"I'm in mourning, actually. I had a Saint Bernard–German shepherd mixed breed dog who died last summer. I know that sounds like a stupid combination, but she was beautiful. All dark shaggy hair and a big face. She was stupid, but she had a great personality. Most people want their dogs to be smart. I think it's more important that they be good-natured, don't you?"

"Misty is not bright," said Bernard, "but she is loyal."

Sarah nodded. She brushed back a tendril of red hair. "Yes. You know what I mean. Loyalty is so important. So few people are loyal. And companionable. My dog's name was Brandy. That sounds a little bit like Misty, doesn't it? Although, not to hurt your feelings, Brandy could have stepped on your dog and never even noticed it. She was huge, and she wasn't well coordinated."

Bernard nodded.

"I like cats, too, but not as much as dogs."

Bernard repressed a shudder. He helped himself to some of the cold cuts that were going around on a large blue-and-white china platter. "I hate cats."

"No—really?"

"Yes. I loathe them."

"Really? And Snooky is so fond of them."

"Yes."

"How does your wife feel about them?"

"She knows I hate them."

"But how does she feel about them?"

"Maya? She loves cats."

Sarah gave him a sly sideways smile, almost feline.

"Then one day you'll probably own one."

Bernard chewed thoughtfully. "Yes. You're probably right." He mused sadly on this for a while. "Do you mind if I give you a little advice?"

"No, of course not. What is it?"

"You seem like a decent person. Why are you going out with Snooky?"

"He told me you would say that," said Sarah, laughing.

"He knows you very well. You don't actually dislike him as much as he says, do you?"

"I like Snooky as much as I like cats. Maybe a little bit less."

Sarah laughed again.

Bernard buried himself in his oversized sandwich and looked covertly around the room. Sarah's aunt Irma, he noted, was making a fool of herself over her young paramour, if that was the right word for it. She was listening to the conversation between Bobby and Maya, and hanging on Bobby's every word. Her wizened hands were constantly in motion, fluttering like leaves, stroking his shoulder, straightening his collar, smoothing down his already overly smooth hair. Bernard scowled to himself. He had nothing against an older woman and a younger man, but the woman was making a fool of herself, fawning on him like that in public. And Bobby Fuller seemed to be just as affectionate in return. He turned to her, including her in the conversation, and put his arm around her. Snooky had his eye on them; so, Bernard thought, did everyone else at the table. Maya was trying to look remote and uninvolved.

"Amazing about Aunt Irma and Bobby, isn't it?" a dry voice asked to his left. He turned to find Dwayne Costa smiling at him mischievously. "They met a few months ago, and apparently it was love at first sight. Hard to believe, eh?"

2 9

Bernard maintained a cautious silence.

"Oh, well," said Dwayne, noticing his reserve. "Not one for gossip, are you? I guess not. Well, good for you. Could you pass the cold cuts, please?"

After the main course came a lemon tart, which Bernard devoured greedily, passing his plate back for seconds and thirds. He was just sitting back with a satisfied grunt, stirring his coffee and cream, when the dining room door flew open and a middle-aged woman came charging in. She was in her late fifties, grotesquely fat, with curly blue hair and an alert, sparkling eye. She was wearing a shapeless gray overcoat over rubber boots. Bernard thought she looked vaguely familiar. Now where had he seen . . . ? Oh, yes, he thought. There was a strong resemblance to several of the dark portraits staring down at them from the walls. There was a heavyset woman over there, for instance, on the wall near the French windows, who despite the portrait's old-fashioned dress could have been her sister. The intruder took up a stance near the head of the table—an almost royal stance—and boomed, "Irma, who the hell are all these people?"

Irma Ditmar rose, her hands fluttering in the air. "Gertie, dear, I told you I was having some people over for lunch—"

"And I wasn't invited again?"

"You were invited, dear. I told you about it yesterday. You said you were going to be on one of your nature walks . . ."

The idea of this Gertie, whoever she was, on a nature walk was enough to give Bernard pause. He felt, uncharitably, that the mere sight of her would frighten away any wildlife and livestock within a hundred miles.

"That's right. So I was," said the mysterious Gertie. She glanced around the table and said, with a nod, "Dwayne."

"Aunt Gertie," replied the young man courteously.

"Bobby."

"Gertrude, how are you?"

"Fine. I found the most marvelous example of *Hydrophyllum* hiding out in the woods behind a tree. It's not in very good shape, of course, but I brought some of it back with me. Have to catalog it in my journals. Have to be scientific, you know. No good being scatterbrained." She delved into the voluminous pockets of her overcoat, then triumphantly produced what looked like a bit of grass. "There. You see?"

Maya was interested. *"Hydrophyllum!* The waterleaf? Surely not at this time of year?"

"Well, of course it's all dried out, but still . . ."

"May I see it?"

The two women moved together and conferred briefly over the herb.

"Fascinating," said Maya. "Note the pinnate toothed leaves."

"Yes, yes. A good one, isn't it?"

"Definitely. I wrote an article about woodland herbs last summer . . ."

"When did this suddenly become a botany seminar?" asked Snooky. "Are we excused from the table, Irma?"

"Yes, dear. You may go now. Sarah, will you help me with the dishes?"

"Of course, Aunt Irma."

Snooky came up to Bernard's side as they left the room and said in a low voice, "That's Gertie Ditmar. Hugo Ditmar's younger sister. Gertie is Irma's sister-in-law. She's been here for years. You noticed the resemblance to the portraits?"

Bernard nodded.

"They're all her relatives," said Snooky. "Ghastly looking bunch, aren't they? Gertie's something else, though. She's always trundling through the woods on her nature hunts. She and Irma are each determined to outlast the other, and gain control of this house. Hugo left it to both of them, with a life interest."

Bernard shrugged irritably. "I don't care, Snooky. Can we leave soon?"

"I'll make up an excuse, and then we can go. Don't say you haven't enjoyed it."

"Why not?"

"Well, the lunch, for one thing. I saw you asking for thirds on that lemon tart."

Snooky, faithful to his word, did make up an excuse a little while later ("It's been wonderful, Irma, thank you so much, but Misty will be climbing the walls if we don't get back soon. I'm sure she's urinated on all the furniture already"), and the three of them left in Bernard's car. Bernard, in the back seat, was silent most of the way home. Maya and Snooky were busy comparing notes about Sarah—"yes, she's very nice, Snookers, I must say I was surprised"—and he felt too stuffed and logy to talk.

"I saw you talking to Dwayne," said Maya at last, turning around in the front seat. "What were the two of you so busy talking about?"

"My writing."

"Mrs. Woolly?"

"No."

"What, then?"

"You know, Maya. My nonfiction works on the history of nuclear power."

"You are terrible," said his wife. "I suppose he believed you?"

"I don't know. I think so."

"Why did you stop there, Bernard?" asked Snooky. "Why didn't you also tell him you wrote *War and Peace*?"

Bernard looked out the window at the passing village of Lyle and tried very hard to forget all the people he had met. He found it exhausting to talk to new people, and his philosophy was, if forced to do it, at least don't brood about it. By the time they reached the cabin, the memory of the luncheon at Hugo's Folly had receded to a dim pinprick in his brain, which was devoting the rest of its function to planning the remainder of his afternoon, in which a cup of hot cider and a nice long nap by the fire figured prominently.

Life at the cabin progressed pleasantly. Bernard found it very comfortable to be a guest in Snooky's household, instead of the other way around, and for his part Snooky was delighted to play host. He went out every afternoon with Maya to do the shopping, and came back loaded with mysterious packages, with which he would disappear into the kitchen for hours. When he reemerged, it was to announce that dinner was ready, and to present his dazzled sister and brother-in-law with one gourmet meal after another. He found a hundred and one things to do with cider, concealing it in stews, vegetable dishes and desserts.

"I bought all this stuff, I have to use it before it goes bad," he would say mournfully, looking at the rows of cider jugs in the back room, behind the kitchen. "I would put it outside, but it would freeze. Have you ever had pumpkin cooked in cider, Maya?"

"No, I don't think so."

"Yes, you did, I made it three days ago. You're not even paying *attention*, Maya. My efforts are wasted on you."

"I never knew Snooky was such a cook," remarked Bernard to his wife one night as they were getting into bed. Misty had discovered that once the fire burned low it was warmer to hide under the quilt, so she had gotten into their bed an hour ago and now greeted them sleepily with a thumping tail.

"Snooky was always a great cook, but he never cooks unless he's in his own home, or whatever passes for that at the time. Anywhere else, he lets people wait on him hand and foot."

"We should always visit *him*."

"I agree absolutely."

"Misty has drooled all over my pillow," Bernard said sadly, holding it up for examination. "At least—oh, God—I hope it's drool."

"Just turn it over and don't think about it. That was some dinner tonight, wasn't it?"

"Yes."

"Snooky said there was cider in the pineapple upside-down cake. Did you taste it?"

"No."

"I didn't either. By the way, sweetheart, how is your work going? Are you getting anything done?"

"I don't know. I can't seem to get off of food. I decided to make it a holiday story. Mrs. Woolly is on vacation and is eating until she suddenly explodes."

"Oh. How is your pillow now? Can you go to sleep?"

"It's fine. G'night, Maya."

"Good night."

A few days later Bernard, contrary to his usual habit, was taking a walk with Misty in the woods. He had gotten frustrated with his writing, since Mrs. Woolly showed no signs of halting her sudden attack of gluttony, so he had gotten out the leash and announced that he was taking a walk. Maya, understanding his mood, had not offered to join him, but had stood at the door reminding him to look human and not get shot.

"And watch out for Misty, too," called Snooky from the kitchen. "Small game season."

The day was bright and lucidly clear, one of those November days where the air seems as brittle as glass. It was so cold that it hurt to breathe. Bernard lumbered morosely through the forest, trying to remember where he was going, since he could imagine nothing worse than getting lost, far from hearth and table and home. Misty, shivering with excitement, bounded ahead of him. On her daily walks with Maya and Snooky she had learned their usual route, and now she picked her way confidently through the trees.

"Misty." Bernard tugged on the leash. "Misty. Come back here. Don't wander away." The leash was a long one that could be wound in like a fishing reel. Shortly after they started, Misty managed to get herself tied securely around a tree. Bernard was cursing and walking in irritable circles, winding in the leash as he went, when there was a snapping and a crackling in the underbrush. A figure came into sight among the trees.

"Ho!" it said.

Bernard looked up. The newcomer was a large man, taller than Bernard, with graying reddish hair and a rugged, thickset face. He was wearing a red-checked flannel shirt, a down vest and khaki-colored trousers and boots. Over his right shoulder was a rifle.

"Ho!" he repeated.

Bernard was not sure how to reply to this. "Hello."

"Lost your beast, eh?"

Bernard disliked him more and more every second. "I haven't lost her. She's gotten tangled up in this tree. I'll have her loose in a minute."

"Ah!" said the hunter. He took his rifle off his shoulder, played with it absently for a minute, slung it back on and said heartily, "Shouldn't let your dog run in the woods, eh? Small game season and all that, you know."

"I know."

"Could be mistaken for a fox."

"I suppose so."

"Of course her hair is too long for a fox. But a lot of people out here, they just shoot anything that moves. You've heard about that, have you?"

"Yes, I have."

"Roger Halberstam," said the stranger, shooting out a meaty hand. "I know you."

"You do?"

"Well, I know of you. You met my stepson the other day. Dwayne, remember? Dwayne Costa? At Irma's? Irma is my sister."

"Oh, yes," said Bernard, reflecting that he had had no choice about meeting Dwayne and family. It seemed too cruel for him to have to meet Dwayne's stepfather as well. "Dwayne. Yes."

"He's out here somewhere, shooting pictures. I hunt with a gun, he hunts with a camera. He's always telling me

3 5

to stop, but I figure, he never brings home anything for dinner, does he now? Does he now?" The man laughed heartily.

"Just don't shoot Misty."

"Oh, no. Wouldn't dream of it. Was that a rabbit? Oh, damn. Never mind. You're Snooky's brother-in-law, are you?"

"Yes. Bernard Woodruff."

"Nice to meet you, Bernard. As I said, be careful in these woods. I'm always telling Dwayne that, too. Can't be too careful these days. Too many crazy people wandering about."

Bernard ground his teeth silently. This was his greatest fear, being played upon by this moronic stranger.

"I'm always telling Dwayne that," repeated Roger Halberstam. Bernard, having freed Misty, began to edge away. "You can't be too careful these days. I keep telling Dwayne to keep his eyes open or he'll get shot. It's happened, you know. Accidents like that do happen."

"I'll be careful."

"Good. Well, nice running into you. Give my best to Snooky. Strange name, isn't it? Snooky. But he seems like a decent young man. Aren't too many of them around these days. Dwayne's another one. As good-hearted as they come. Not much of a wage-earner, of course, but that can't be helped. I think he has some talent, myself. He just hasn't found what it is, exactly."

"Yes," said Bernard. "How interesting. Good-bye."

"Good-bye. If you run into Dwayne lurking around here with his camera, tell him to be home before dark. I worry about him, you know. I worry about that boy. He's like my own son."

"Good-bye."

"Good-bye," said Roger Halberstam. He stared for a moment after the rapidly retreating figures of Bernard and Misty, then hefted his gun in his hands and started back the other way through the woods.

2

"I have some bad news for you, Bernard," said Snooky. "Steel yourself."

"What is it?"

Snooky sat down on the sofa opposite him. "I've invited Sarah and her family over here for dinner tomorrow night."

Bernard lifted up his red pencil and made a mark on the page in the typewriter before him.

"I know you're not happy about it, but I wanted to reciprocate for that lunch the other day. Just say you won't leave."

Bernard took the page out of the typewriter and looked at it thoughtfully.

"I discussed it with Maya, and she says you'll probably stick around for the food. She said the best way was just to tell you straight out, so that's what I'm doing. I know that deep down, inside that gruff and silent exterior, you appreciate my honesty."

Bernard grunted.

"They'll be here around six-thirty. I wanted you to

know. I know that cuts into your predinner snack, but remember: it's just one evening."

Bernard shrugged and picked irritably at the remains of last night's peach cobbler, which was sitting next to him in a battered pie tin.

"Well, that wasn't so bad," said Snooky cheerfully, rising to his feet.

"What are you going to cook?"

"Whatever you want."

"Beef stew."

"Beef stew? Bernard, I've made beef stew practically every night since you and Maya arrived. Don't you ever get tired of it?"

"No."

"All that red meat. It's bad for you, you know."

"I know."

"All right. Beef stew it is. Beef stew with my secret ingredient."

"That would be cider," said Bernard.

"Yes."

"Slightly rancid cider."

"Yes."

"How bad does it have to be before you finally throw it away?"

"I don't know. All I know is, it's not there yet. I'm going to send in Maya to talk to you now. Kind of a pre-party therapy session. Thank you again for your time and attention."

He went back into the kitchen, and shortly thereafter Maya came out, holding two cups of steaming cider. She handed one to Bernard and sat down next to him, entwining her fingers in his. "How're you doing?"

"Well, for one thing, if I have to drink any more of this cider, I'm going to throw up."

"There are only two jugs left."

"Didn't Snooky make any coffee?"

"No. You're in a good mood."

Bernard snarled at her.

"You'll survive this party," said Maya absently. She sipped her drink and gazed around the room. "It's just one evening."

"That's what your brother said."

"Snooky is knocking himself out to make your favorite meal for everybody."

"So what?"

"So he's making an effort."

"Fine." Bernard drank his cider and lapsed into a gloomy silence. Maya regarded him, a smile playing around the corners of her lips.

"How're things with Mrs. Woolly?"

"I can't work with all these interruptions." Bernard got up, dislodging Misty, who was asleep on his feet. Misty's tail thumped once, then she crept closer to the fire and fell asleep again. Bernard paced irritably up and down the room. "I don't find Sarah and her family particularly interesting. I never do find Snooky's girlfriends interesting. I don't see why I have to socialize with them. I don't see why they have to come here, where I happen to be living right now. I don't know how I'm going to get any work done between now and then. You know it throws me off for days if I have to see anyone."

"I know."

Bernard sat back down and slurped his cider angrily. "Can we go home soon? Misty is homesick."

Maya glanced at Misty, who was snoring happily, curled up into a little ball. "Yes. Misty looks homesick. We'd better get her back to Connecticut before she keels over. Have you ever thought that maybe you would get more work done if you had less time to do it in?"

"Thank you very much."

"One more thing. Snooky would like to make your favorite dessert tomorrow. He asked me what it was, and I couldn't think."

"No, Maya. No. Tell him I can't be bribed."

"But I've already told him you could."

"Oh, all right," said Bernard. "In that case, tell him I'd

like that apple walnut pie he makes. The one with the crumbly topping."

"Now you're making sense. Did I ever tell you that you are the most rotten traveler in the world?" She leaned over, gave him a kiss, then vanished into the kitchen, from which Bernard could soon hear the sounds of muffled laughter. He turned back to his work. Mrs. Woolly was being particularly difficult. Right now she was eating peach cobbler and spitting the crumbs all over the devoted cadre of children who followed her around. He read over what he had written, sighed deeply and picked up his red pencil.

"Have you seen Bernard's face?" Maya asked her brother the next evening. "I think he just died."

Snooky was scraping the beef stew into a casserole dish. He arranged boiled quartered red potatoes and carrots carefully around the outside, sprinkled them with paprika and put some sprigs of parsley on top. "I know. And the evening's barely begun."

"He'll be all right."

"I put him next to Sarah. He seemed to enjoy talking to her last time."

"I don't think the problem is Sarah," said Maya, peeking out the kitchen door. "I think it's that new guy—Roger. Roger Halberstam. Bernard met him in the woods the other day and said he was strange."

"Well, he *is* strange."

"He sat down on the other side of Bernard before I could stop him."

"It's good for him," Snooky said cheerfully. "Here, Maya. Take in this dish of vegetables while I carry in the stew. You know I've always told you Bernard should get out and mix a little more. You know, mellow his character a bit."

"Bernard doesn't need to be mellowed, Snooky. He's fine the way he is."

"Yes, well, there are conflicting opinions on that. Here are the vegetables. We'll come back for the pumpkin dish."

At the table, Roger Halberstam, his large meaty features aglow, was talking about a rabbit he had killed the previous day. "Skinny little feller," he was saying, gesturing with his hands. "Not much fat on him. Fast, though. Faster than I expected. He scurried off into the bushes before I got my gun up. But I waited, and he came out again. That's when I blew his head off. Rabbits are fast," he concluded thoughtfully, "but they're not very smart."

There was a silence around the table.

"Charming little story," said Bobby Fuller finally, lifting up his wineglass. "Thank you for that interesting piece of natural history."

"Roger, I wish you wouldn't talk about your hunting at the dinner table," Irma said fretfully. She was wearing a stylishly designed red velvet dress tonight, a dress whose sleek lines made her look older, not younger. She wore an expensive strand of milk-white pearls and matching pearl earrings. Once again she had too much makeup on, her lips a shade too red, her eyes outlined in dusky brown. She sat next to Bobby, her gaze wandering protectively over him. "You know how it upsets everybody."

"Don't see why," responded her brother. "Don't see why."

"Please, Roger."

"All right, Irmie."

At the other end of the table, the huge fat woman whom Bernard recalled vaguely as Gertie Ditmar gave a loud snort. She was dressed tonight in shapeless tweeds and large, obviously artificial pearls. "Hunters have no respect for the environment."

"That's not true," replied Roger. "We have a great deal of respect for the environment. Do you know how many deer would die of starvation if they weren't hunted anyway?"

"Oh, shut up, Roger. You don't know what you're talking about. You have no—no *respect* for living things."

"Hmmmppphh," said Roger. He and Gertie glared at each other for a moment. Then he lifted the serving bowl

4 1

filled with stew and said, "Hey, this looks great. Look at this. What's everybody else going to eat, ha ha ha?"

Across the table, Dwayne winced.

Next to Bernard, Sarah put a soft hand on his. She said in a low voice, "Don't let Uncle Roger get to you. He does the gruff English squire bit, but he's different from that underneath, he really is. He's been a wonderful father to Dwayne ever since Dwayne's mother died. And Dwayne's not even his own son."

Bernard silently helped himself to the stew.

"Dwayne told me you wrote a bestseller about nuclear power plants," Sarah said. She smiled, a dimple showing briefly. "That's a lie, isn't it?"

"Yes."

"You've never written about power plants?"

"No."

"You *are* mean. He's been telling everybody. He loved the thought of meeting a bestselling author."

Bernard shrugged.

Sarah tilted her head to one side, looking at him. She was wearing a simple black wool dress with a red belt. Her hair was drawn back smoothly and gathered at the nape of her neck, and she wore tiny diamond earrings that sparkled with brilliant colors in the candlelight. Snooky flopped down next to her. "How's the food?" he asked.

"Delicious."

"Liar. You haven't even tried it yet. Bernard has been keeping you too busy with his witty repartee. Haven't you, Bernard?"

Bernard picked up his fork and began to eat.

"You see?" said Snooky.

At first, everyone around the table had a communal conversation; but soon, under the influence of food and wine, the talk broke up into pairs and trios, leaving Bernard isolated in a conversational vacuum. He was perfectly content. He busied himself with a third and fourth helping of the stew and the pumpkin dish. He kept the butter plate conveniently nearby, for the excellent French bread that Snooky was passing around, and studiously avoided any attempts on the part of his dinner companions to engage him in conversation. As the dinner progressed, he rose out of his preoccupation with the meal and began to notice an undercurrent of—could it be hostility or unease?—around the table. Irma was being, as before, overly affectionate with her young paramour, and it was drawing unfavorable glances and critical whispers. Everything Bobby said was brilliant; she hung on his every word; he knew best about everything. Bernard, watching the unlikely pair, thought that she appeared to be genuinely in love with him. What the young man felt was, of course, another matter. He seemed to be a little more withdrawn tonight than at lunch the other day; but perhaps he was simply more aware than she was of the amused, contemptuous looks they were receiving.

Bernard went back to his dinner with an inward shrug of indifference. It didn't matter to him what Irma Ditmar decided to do with her life and her money. If she wanted to make a fool of herself over a younger man, that was her business. And perhaps Bobby liked her for more than just her wealth. There was no telling. He glanced covertly sideways at his brother-in-law. Snooky was, unlike the others, paying no attention to Irma's fussing and demonstrations of affection. He was clearing the dishes and chattering to Maya, but there was a thoughtful, inward look on his face.

"Poor Aunt Irma," Sarah said in a half-whisper at Bernard's side. She was buttering her bread with short, angry gestures. "It's ridiculous, isn't it? Irma's always been foolish over younger men, ever since Hugo died. But this one is more serious than the others."

"If it makes her happy, who cares?"

"Well, there's a bit more to it than that—" Sarah started to say, when Snooky emerged from the kitchen with a steaming deep dish apple pie. "Look at that!" she said in admiration.

Bernard was already looking.

"This dessert is at Bernard's request," Snooky said. "Apple walnut pie with a crumb topping. Here's the cream." He served huge slices slathered in heavy cream and topped with chopped walnuts. There were oohs and aahs around the table.

Roger Halberstam looked as if he had died and gone to heaven. "Delicious," he said between forkfuls. "Absolutely delicious."

Gertie, at the end of the table, was already gesturing for more and talking to Bobby in a loud voice. "I was out in the woods the other day," she was saying, "and I saw a black squirrel. I didn't know there were any this far north. A black squirrel, I'm telling you. A delightful little creature. You should spend more time in the woods, Bobby," she said severely. "You're so pale. It would be good for you."

"I don't get much time off, Gertie. You know that."

"Ah, yes, that law firm you work in. Slave drivers. Anyway, as I was saying . . ."

"You're a lawyer?" Maya asked.

"A law clerk, I'm afraid," Bobby said. "A paralegal. We work just as hard but don't make as much money."

"I see."

"That's how we met," Irma chirped up, her cheeks a bright pink. "Bobby works for my lawyer, Mr. Estes of Estes, Wolf and Harrison. Don't you, dear?"

"I certainly do."

"What's he like, Bobby?" asked Dwayne.

"As Gertie says. A slave driver."

Irma began to fuss. "I know, poor dear. I've spoken to him about it several times, but it never seems to make any difference. I think he works you far too hard."

"Oh, it doesn't matter, Irma."

"Yes, it does. It does, Bobby. It matters to me. I hate to see you all pale and wan-looking, like Gertie said. You should get out more."

"I get out plenty."

"No, you don't, poor dear." Irma subsided into chirps of birdlike pleasure as Snooky handed her a plate of pie and cream. "Oh, my. This is lovely. Thank you so much. Where did your brother learn to cook like this, Maya?"

4 4

Maya was disemboweling her pie and looking at it critically. "I have no idea. Nobody ever taught him. It's just one of his little gifts. He's gifted in the most unexpected ways, most of them not terribly useful. What are these, Snooky? Currants?"

"Yes, My. They had some in the store, so I threw them in."

"I can taste the cider," Bernard pronounced gloomily.

Snooky served out the coffee in large French cups with a delicate floral pattern. "Nice cups, aren't these? I found them in the back of the cupboard. I'm probably not supposed to be using them. Cream or sugar?"

Once everyone had their coffee, and the first slices of pie had disappeared, Irma rose slowly from the table, supporting herself on Bobby's shoulder. She lifted up her half-empty wineglass. "Listen, everyone," she said tremulously. "Please listen. I have the most wonderful announcement to make."

The conversation, which had been running in subdued rivulets around the table, was immediately stilled.

Irma gripped Bobby's shoulder tightly, and her cheeks turned an unhealthy shade of red. Under the heavy makeup, she actually seemed to be blushing.

"Bobby and I . . ." She faltered, her voice quivering. "Bobby and I . . . oh, *dear* . . . well, we've decided to get *married!*"

There was a moment of dead silence. Then everyone began to talk at once. Sarah went around and kissed her aunt. Dwayne shook Bobby's hand heartily. Gertie looked vastly amused and kept on eating her dessert as if nothing at all had happened.

Roger stood up and threw his arms around his sister. "Why, Irmie, you old fox! How long have you been planning this? My God, Bobby, you're a lucky guy!" He shook Bobby's hand. "When's the date? Have the two of you set a date?"

"Wait till the spring," said Gertie. "There's nothing like a spring wedding."

"Oh, dear . . . oh, no . . . I don't know," twittered Irma. "We haven't even discussed it yet."

"Well, you'll have to stop keeping all these secrets and let us in on your plans," Roger said. "Hey? Do you hear what I'm saying, Irmie?"

"Of course, Roger."

"So happy for you both," said Roger heartily. He wrung Bobby's hand again and sat down. But Bernard, next to him, noticed that as he picked up his napkin and spread it carefully over his lap, his hands were shaking.

"Why did she have to pick *my* dinner party to make that announcement?" mourned Snooky. He and Maya were clearing the table later that evening. Everyone had left half an hour before, in a flurry of thanks and slightly inebriated good-byes.

"I noticed how happy the whole family was."

"It ruined everything. It ruined everything, Maya. I had the whole evening planned so carefully. We were going to sit in front of the fire and tell stories. It was all going so well, wasn't it? And then she springs that announcement. Oh, damn."

"Forgive me for asking," said Bernard from his seat by the fire, "but what business is it of her family's if she decides to remarry?"

"It's something you wouldn't understand, Bernard. It's a worldly concern. Something that someone like you wouldn't comprehend. It has to do with money."

"What about money?"

"Irma is rich, Bernard. Rich beyond your wildest dreams. Her husband left her everything except for a half-share of the house, which he gave to his sister Gertie. But Gertie didn't get any money, just a life interest in the house. And nobody else got anything at all. They're all dependent on Irma in one way or another. Roger thought he was an entrepreneur, like Hugo, but all his businesses failed one after another. Sarah said it was pathetic, how he would come to Irma and Hugo—and now just Irma—with his hat in his hand, asking for money. Anyway, how do you think they would all feel if Irma marries again and leaves her fortune to Bobby? They're only human, Bernard. They've got to be disappointed." Snooky balanced three plates on top of each other with an angry clatter.

Bernard had lost interest long ago. He sat gazing happily into the fire.

"He's not listening to me. He never does listen to me. I could yell 'Fire!' and he wouldn't hear," Snooky told his sister.

"Don't take it personally, Snooks. You know better than that. It's the way he is."

"Will you help me with the dishes, My?"

"Sure."

They went into the kitchen, leaving Bernard far away in his reveries.

A few days later Bernard and Misty were tracing their usual path among the trees. It was a bitterly cold day. Their breath billowed like white clouds before their faces. It had snowed heavily the night before, and their tracks fled away behind them, stretching back as a tangible link to the cabin. Bernard was not in a good mood. He had begun to suspect that he was putting on weight. Not much, of course—he never did gain much—but enough. Maya, after breakfast that morning, had glanced at his waistline critically. "Sweetheart, maybe you'd better take the dog for a walk." Snooky had agreed. "Yes, Bernard, why don't you take Misty out today? It would do you good." Bernard had protested furiously, but to no avail. Here he was, trudging along, bundled up in his down coat against the frigid cold.

Misty seemed delighted, as always, to be outdoors. The cold did not seem to bother her. She bounded along, sniffing eagerly at invisible objects. Bernard followed behind, a dark glowering bundle of heavy clothes and scarves. The cold usually did not bother him either—he went outdoors in the winter with just a light coat on—but this did not qualify as merely "cold." It was, he decided as he walked along, arctic hell. He had had to break the ice in the sink this morning. It was more than time enough to be heading home. Surely they had put in enough time in Snooky's cabin. His thoughts lingered luxuriously on central heating.

Misty gave a peculiar little yelp and strained forward at the end of the leash. Bernard pulled her back irritably. She ran around in circles, winding herself neatly around a bush, then disappeared. Bernard cursed and followed her.

"What is it, Misty? Misty? Come back here, you . . . what is it?"

When he finally found her, she was sniffing at something half-hidden under the bush.

"What is it?" he asked irritably. It was a large dark object. Visions of half-dead animals, of hunters and deer, of Roger Halberstam's unfortunate rabbit, floated through his mind. He began to unwind the leash from the bush.

"What *is* it, Misty? Come here right now."

Misty, like most faithful dogs, paid no attention to what he was saying. She whined and surged forward on the leash.

"Oh, all right," said Bernard in disgust. He followed her around the back of the bush. There was something on the ground there, half-buried in the ice and snow . . . was it an animal? Bernard shut his eyes, shuddered, then leaned forward to look.

"We're going to have to put him on a diet," Snooky was saying at that very moment. He and Maya sat on opposite couches, their legs stretched out toward the fire, steaming cups of cider next to them. "A diet, Maya. There's no other way. He's getting really hefty."

"Bernard always gains weight in the winter. He's like a bear."

"Or a squirrel."

"Whatever. He loses it naturally in the spring. Bernard is very much in tune with the seasons." Maya sipped her drink. "You know, Snooky, Bernard is right. This stuff could make you sick. It's gone off already."

"Not yet, Maya. Not yet. And it's almost finished, you

know. Do you realize by the time you leave we'll have used up twenty gallons?"

"What on earth possessed you to rush out and buy twenty gallons?"

"I don't know, My. I had just arrived here, and I lost my head. I thought it was the most delicious thing I had ever tasted in my life. It's fresh from the orchards."

"Well, all I can say is that you've turned me off the stuff forever. When we get back to Connecticut, I hope I never see a drop of it again." Maya looked up as the door opened and her husband came in. "Oh, there you are, sweetheart. How was your walk?"

"We were just talking about you, Bernard. We were just saying that it's time you went on a little—"

"Wait a minute," said Maya. Bernard had taken off his big bulky hat and she had seen his face. "Sweetheart? What's wrong?"

Bernard headed for the nearest chair, Misty trailing behind him, and sat down heavily.

"I have seen something bad," he said.

Maya reached over and took his hand. "What is it?"

"Somebody has to call the police," Bernard said. "Bobby Fuller has been shot to death in the woods."

3

Detective Larry Bentley of the Wolfingham police force
was, Bernard reflected, not so much big as just plain mean.
He was very short but very wide, and he somehow con-
veyed an impression of toughness and durability, like raw-
hide. He had a square face with piggy features and small
squinty eyes. His dark thinning hair was combed carefully
over a bald spot in back. He was not someone whom Bernard would ordinarily invite as a house guest, and he
wished very fervently that Detective Bentley was not sitting in the living room of the cabin right now.

"I don't understand, Mr. Woodruff," said Detective Bentley. "What were you doing out in the woods?"

"I was taking a walk."

"Right." The thought of anyone, particularly a visitor,
taking a walk on a sunny November day in the Vermont
woods seemed to strain the detective's power of imagination. "With your dog?"

"Yes."

"This dog?" He made a vague gesture with his foot.

"Of course this dog. Do you see any other dogs around here?"

"Now, now, Mr. Woodruff. It's my job, you know, asking questions. It doesn't do any good to blow up. I might have to take you down to the station for questioning. So you were walking with your dog in the section of the woods you showed me earlier, and . . . ?" He waited with his pen hovering in the air.

"As I told you before, Misty began to sniff around that bush. She got herself wound around it, and while I was unwinding her, I saw something lying in the snow. Something large and dark. It was half-buried, so it took me a while to figure out what it was."

"And it was . . . ?"

"A package from Peking," said Bernard. "Do we have to go through all this again? It was Bobby Fuller's body. He was lying there, shot through the head."

"Mmmmm." Detective Bentley was writing furiously. He ripped the top page off his pad and crumpled it up in his pocket. "Hmmmm. Yes. And then you—?"

"Went to the moon."

Bentley looked up reproachfully. "Mr. Woodruff."

"Took a nice walk, enjoying the woods covered with snow."

"Mr. Woodruff."

"Came right back here to the cabin and had Snooky call you," said Bernard irritably. "Why, I can't imagine. It doesn't seem that anything is getting done."

"All in good time, Mr. Woodruff. All in good time." Detective Bentley nodded his thick meaty head. The hair over his bald spot flopped back and forth as if possessed by a will of its own. Snooky found himself staring at it, fascinated. *I wonder if I'll start doing that when I go bald,* he thought, grasping his full head of light brown hair in sudden appreciation. His thoughts drifted off into apprehensive visions of a balding future, while Bentley's voice receded gently into a background drone. Bernard's voice punctuated the drone with short, angry rumbles. *I wonder how I'll look*, thought Snooky, sprawled next to the hearth. *I wonder if I'll still be good-looking* . . .

Maya was thinking, *This man really is a pig. I wonder if we can serve him some of that cider?*

When Snooky dreamily tuned in again, Bernard was trembling with rage and saying in a strangled voice, "That's all I know. That is all I know. That is *all* I know. That is all I *know*."

"Now, now, Mr. Woodruff. Just doing my job. Don't put on that tone of voice with me. So that's all you know?"

Bernard did not reply.

Bentley scribbled something down. "You knew Bobby Fuller, didn't you?"

"Yes. He had dinner here three days ago. He and a bunch of other people."

"A bunch of other people?"

Bernard enumerated.

"They had dinner here?" Bentley looked around the cabin.

"Yes."

"All those people?"

"Yes."

"What did they eat?"

Bernard refused to answer this. Snooky said, "A really delicious beef stew. I made it myself."

"This is your cabin?"

"Yes. Well, I'm renting it while the owners are away. They're in France. Lyons, actually. They have some sort of business there. The lady who owns this cabin is half-French. Their name is Wuxler. Patrick and Marie Wuxler. I can give you their address in Lyons, if you like, but I'm afraid they wouldn't be much help. They've been out of the country for nearly two months now."

"I see." The detective rose to his full height of just over five feet. "I'll be seeing you around, Mr. Woodruff."

Bernard nodded.

Bentley pocketed his pad of paper and left. They could hear his ancient yellow car, parked in front of the picket fence, cough slowly to life and move away down the dirt path.

"I try to do my civic duty," said Bernard. "I find a body, and I report it. And I get treated like a common criminal for doing so."

"Yes," said Snooky. "And that's Wolfingham's finest you're looking at."

"Why Wolfingham?"

"It's the big town around here. Lyle doesn't have its own police force."

"Neither, apparently, does Wolfingham," said Bernard. "Is there any cake left over from last night?"

"Yes," said Snooky.

"Bring it out here to me."

Snooky came back with a big slice of lemon cake. Bernard placed it in front of him, cut it neatly in two and forked half of it into his mouth. Maya regarded him worriedly.

"You shouldn't eat for comfort, darling. It's so bad for you."

"I'm not eating for comfort. I'm angry."

"You shouldn't eat because you're angry."

"All right, I'm not angry. I'm hungry. I had a long, pleasant walk in the woods today, and now I'm hungry."

"Somebody's going to have to break the news to Sarah," said Snooky. "She's the one who should tell Irma about it. She'll know what to do."

Maya stared out the window. "Do you think all those men are still there?" The detective had brought a group of men who had tramped off into the woods with Bernard and Snooky to examine the body and the surrounding area.

"Probably," said Snooky. "I heard the medical examiner say that he was shot yesterday afternoon. Then it snowed on him last night."

5 3

There was a short silence at this bleak image. Maya crossed her arms. "The poor man."

Snooky picked up the telephone and dialed rapidly. "Hello? Who's this? Gertie, it's Snooky. Is Sarah there? No? Oh. Well, Gertie, I have some bad news. Is Irma there? All right. You'd better be the one to tell her. I'm terribly sorry, but Bobby Fuller is dead . . . What? . . . Dead. Yes. He was . . . well, he was shot to death in the woods . . . What? . . . No, they don't know whether it was a hunting accident . . . Yes, I know those hunters are crazy. Anyway, somebody's going to have to break it to Irma . . . all right. All right. I wanted to warn you. The detective from Wolfingham is on his way over, and he's an idiot, so I wanted you to know . . . Okay. Please have Sarah call me when she can . . . Thanks. Bye." He put the phone down. "Well, that wasn't easy. I hate those kind of calls."

"Those kind of calls?" said Maya. "What do you mean? Have you ever had to make one before?"

"No, but—you remember, My—I've received them."

Maya's face changed. It lost its angularity and became much softer. She crossed the room to put an arm around his shoulder. "Oh. I'm sorry, Snooks. Of course you have."

When Snooky was five years old, he had been alone in the house when the call had come through about their parents' car accident. The well-meaning but moronic relative who had called to offer sympathy had given it to him, not realizing that the family had not yet heard.

"We should go over to the house and offer our condolences," said Snooky.

"We should bring something," said Maya. "Flowers, perhaps."

"We should get in our car," said Bernard, "and drive very quickly back to Connecticut."

Later, with Maya and Snooky busy in the kitchen, Bernard sat by the fire in a pensive mood. That terrible moment of realization when he was bending over Bobby Fuller's frozen body . . . he shuddered. He had not known the man—he had only met him twice—but he felt sorry for

5 4

him. Whatever he had done, surely he did not deserve to die alone in the woods and be left for carrion. Surely he did not deserve that.

The Grunwald sisters were the happiest they had been in years. There is nothing like a murder in a small town to give the elderly residents a new lease on life. Alicia and Charlotte, once they heard the news, retired to their sitting room to rejoice. They were two tall, beak-nosed spinsters, with gray faces and gray eyes and gray hair. They had managed to receive a strict Victorian upbringing in twentieth-century America. Their father had been a minister, and in all their lives they had traveled no farther than the neighboring town of Wolfingham. A murder—an actual *murder*—in Lyle, in their lifetimes, had seemed too much to hope for. They sat together and twittered.

"This is terrible news," said Alicia, the older sister.

"Terrible," agreed Charlotte.

"Poor Irma," said Alicia, tucking back a strand of gray hair. She had been horribly jealous of Irma Ditmar and her young lover. In her few quiet moments, she admitted this to herself. But now there was no need to be jealous, simply sympathetic, which was *so* much easier to handle. Alicia herself had never had a young lover, even when she herself was young.

"Poor Irma!" repeated Charlotte.

"Those hunters. There should be a law."

"A law, yes."

"Would you care for some tea?"

"Yes, thank you, Alicia."

Charlotte, pale echo of her sister, was three years younger but looked just as aged. She was only a few years older than Irma Ditmar, and had been even more jealous of her than her sister. "Terrible for the family," she said now. *"Terrible."*

"Terrible!" Alicia said cheerfully. She paused, tea kettle in hand. "When do you think we should go over there and comfort her, the poor thing?"

5 5

"Oh, not yet. Not right now. It's too soon."

"I suppose you're right." Alicia poured out carefully for both of them. "There you are. Two sugars. There's the doorbell. Why don't you get it?"

Charlotte was towed back into the room by a vigorous white-haired gentleman with a still-handsome face and bright blue eyes.

"Frank," Alicia greeted him. "Have a seat. Some tea?"

He accepted a cup. "You've heard the news?"

"About poor Irma's friend? Sadly, yes."

"Knock it off, Alicia. You and your sister here have been plotting Irma's death for years. You've never liked her, and you're not sorry for her now."

"That's not true. Irma is one of my dearest friends."

The elderly man snorted. He drank his tea in a gulp and stood up. "If it makes you feel any better, the rest of the town's old biddies are the same way. Every one of them was jealous of Irma and her catch."

Charlotte sniffed loudly. "It was indecent. The man was thirty years younger."

"Yes, well, somebody took care of that." The old man's glittering blue eyes swept over the two sisters. "Somebody took care of that, didn't they?"

"Don't look at us that way, Mr. Frank Vanderwoort," said Alicia stiffly. "It was an accident—a hunting accident. I heard that on good authority."

"Gertie, huh?" said the old man shrewdly. "I saw the two of you whispering out back a little while ago. Gertie's not that stupid, and neither are you. I don't think it was an accident."

"Not . . . not an accident?" faltered Charlotte.

"No, my dear girl. It was murder, plain and simple. I'd watch what you say for the next few days. The police are sniffing all around town, looking for clues. Not that the two of you know anything. You may be old dried-up spinsters, but you're not murderers, that's for sure."

"There's no need to be offensive, Frank," said Alicia mildly. "You're not exactly in the bloom of youth yourself."

He let out a snuffling snort of laughter. "No, by God, but if I were, I'd give you a runaround, kid!" He slapped her familiarly on the back and left. It was as if a whirlwind had swept through the parlor. Alicia found her hair was disarranged. She tucked it neatly behind her ear and turned excitedly to her sister.

"Charlotte, he's right! It was a murder—a *real* murder—not an accident!"

There followed a small sensation in the sitting room of the Grunwald house.

Snooky had been at Hugo's Folly during the afternoon. Now, as the light faded from the sky, he sat in the living room of the cabin, hugging a pillow to his chest, and told Maya and Bernard all about it.

"Sarah's fine. She doesn't seem very upset. None of them do, actually, except Irma. She had to be put to bed with an elephant dose of tranquilizers. Poor woman. She wanted to come and see the body, but she was too weak. I didn't think it was a good idea, myself. Letting her see the body, I mean. She's had enough of a shock as it is."

"Who else is at the house?" asked Maya.

"The whole family. Dwayne and his stepfather and Sarah and Gertie. Dwayne and Roger came over as soon as they heard. And some friends from the village have been stopping by."

"Do they still think it was a hunting accident?"

"I don't know, Maya. Detective Bentley hasn't told me."

"Very convenient that he would be murdered right after the wedding announcement," said Bernard.

"Yes."

"Doesn't look too good for the family."

"No, it doesn't."

"Of course," said Bernard, "with Detective Bentley on the case, whoever did it doesn't have to worry much about being caught."

"True." Snooky leaned back thoughtfully on the sofa. "I'm worried about Sarah. She's close to her aunt, and once

Irma wakes up there's going to be a scene. I wouldn't be surprised if this killed her. Irma, I mean. Her heart isn't very strong."

Bernard recalled the layers of makeup which obscured her real color. "How can you tell?"

"Sarah told me. She could go at any time. The shock might kill her."

"Maybe that's what somebody is hoping for."

Snooky sucked in his lips between his teeth. "You have a very nasty mind, Bernard. I compliment you on it."

"Thank you."

"He's realistic," Maya said warmly, putting an arm around her husband. "Bernard has always been the soul of practicality."

"Plus, he hates people, so he always thinks the worst."

"Yes."

"You're right, of course, Bernard. That could indeed be what somebody is hoping for." Snooky went to the window and gazed out at the fast-vanishing afternoon. "Danger. Danger. Red alert. Bentley approaching at ten o'clock, in that old yellow crate of his. Fifty meters to go."

"Coming to arrest me, no doubt," Bernard said bitterly. "I'll go quietly."

"Thirty meters."

"This will teach me never to take a walk in the woods. I knew I shouldn't go. Didn't I, Maya? Didn't I say I didn't want to go that day?"

"Yes, you did, sweetheart."

"Ten meters."

"I've changed my mind," said Bernard. "I won't go without a fight. They'll have to drag me down to the police station." He settled back with a resigned expression as Bentley came in the door. The detective grunted hello, sat down opposite Bernard and unveiled a long cloth-covered object with a flourish. It was a rifle.

"Do you know what this is, Mr. Woodruff?"

Bernard gazed at it in silence for a long time. "A space ship."

58

"No."

"A champagne fountain."

"No."

"A ticket for me and my wife for a free trip to Paris."

"It's a rifle, Mr. Woodruff. Is it yours?"

"No."

"Are you sure?"

"Positive."

"You've never seen it before?"

Bernard hesitated.

"Aha!" said Bentley in triumph. "You *have* seen it. Where?"

"Wait a minute," said Bernard. "Where did you find it?"

"It was in the woods, not a hundred yards from the body. No fingerprints on it, of course. No footprints anywhere, because of the snow. But once I find out who it belongs to, I'll know who killed Bobby Fuller. We also found Fuller's car parked by the woods, on the road into Lyle. He must have left it there when he went for his little walk. Clear as glass, isn't it?"

"Are you sure?"

"About what?"

"That whoever owns that rifle killed Bobby with it?"

"Of course I am. And even if the owner didn't do it, it narrows the field, doesn't it? Now tell me, where have you seen it?"

"I don't know," said Bernard. "I can't tell one gun from another. I'm not a gun expert."

"Come on, Mr. Woodruff. You recognized it, didn't you? It's a Winchester 30-caliber, used for hunting. And it has this scratch here." The detective indicated a deep wavering line along the stock. "Where have you seen it?"

Bernard hesitated. He said slowly, "I'm not sure, but . . . Roger Halberstam had a gun like that."

"Roger Halberstam?"

"When I met him in the woods. He was carrying a rifle . . . it could be the same one. I can't say for sure. All guns look alike to me."

"Thank you, Mr. Woodruff," said the detective. He stood up, smiling. "Thank you very much."

"Good-bye, Detective."

"Good-bye."

After Bentley had left, Bernard turned to Maya. "I may just have implicated an innocent man," he said heavily.

"He may have done it, sweetheart."

"Maya, if you were going to murder someone, would you use your own rifle and then throw it away less than a hundred yards from the body, for anybody to find?"

"Maybe," said Snooky. "To throw everybody off. It's obvious that it's a stupid thing to do, right? So maybe it would confuse everyone."

"It doesn't seem to have confused Detective Bentley. He's sure it's Roger Halberstam who did it."

"No proof," said Snooky.

"He thinks the gun is proof."

"He can think whatever he wants. He doesn't have any real proof. Even if it *does* belong to Roger, anybody in the family could have taken that gun."

"And someone probably did," said Bernard dryly.

"Damn it," said Roger a quarter of an hour later. He was sitting in the living room of Hugo's Folly. The light glittering off the snow outside made the silver frames, mirrors and shiny gewgaws painfully bright. "Damn it. I mean, *damn* it. Yes, it's my rifle. But anybody could have taken it. I mean, I haven't seen it for *days.* I haven't been out hunting."

"Where do you usually keep it?" asked Bentley.

"In my hall closet at home, near the front door."

"You haven't used it? For how long?"

"Oh, at least three or four days. Since that dinner at the cabin. Everyone made such a fuss about my hunting, I decided to lay off for a while. Besides, it's been damn cold. Damn cold."

"I see."

"That's the truth, I'm telling you. The truth. Ask Dwayne. He knows I haven't been out in the woods. Actually, he's been there himself, shooting."

"Shooting?"

Roger let out a shaky wuffle of laughter. "Sorry. Shooting pictures. He's by way of being an amateur photographer."

"You say anyone could have taken the rifle?"

"Yes, damn it. Nobody locks their houses around here. Anyone could have come in during the last couple of days and taken it right out of the closet. It's no secret that I own one."

"No," said the detective, his piggy eyes narrowing, "but not everyone would know where it was kept, would they? Can you tell me who would know that?"

"Well," said Roger slowly, "anyone in the family, I guess. They probably know where I keep the gun, they've seen me take it out when I go hunting. Maybe some of the neighbors."

"Who are your neighbors?"

"The Grunwald sisters on one side, Frank Vanderwoort on the other."

Bentley wrote this down. "What was Bobby Fuller doing in the woods outside of town late yesterday afternoon, do you think? He didn't usually go in for walks like that, did he?"

"No. I don't know why he suddenly decided to be there. He didn't call me up beforehand and ask my advice. I do know that at dinner the other night, some of the women were nagging him, telling him to get out more. That it would be good for him, you know. I find it that way myself. Salubrious. A brisk walk in the woods, don't you know, on the lookout for game."

"Who was telling him to get out more?"

"Oh, damn it . . . I don't know. Gertie brought it up, I guess, and then my sister agreed with her. They said he was working too hard and should get out more. I think maybe

Sarah put in her two cents also. Maybe he listened to them. Maybe he had a rendezvous with someone. How would I know? We weren't friendly."

"Where were you, Mr. Halberstam, yesterday afternoon?"

"I was home all day," Roger said readily. "Ask anyone. Ask Dwayne. Oh no, damn it, Dwayne was out. Well, I don't know if I have any goddamned witnesses for my goddamned alibi. The truth of the matter is, I was home, watching television. It had snowed and I thought it was too cold to go out. I told Dwayne so, but he wouldn't listen."

"Thank you, Mr. Halberstam. Don't go anywhere, by the way. We'll have our eye on you."

"Perish the thought," Roger said jovially. He rose to his feet. "Is the interview over? May I leave?"

"Yes, thank you."

"I'll try not to kill anyone else while you're around," said Roger, in a ghastly attempt at humor. He crossed the room to stand at the door. "It would be stupid of me to try that with your hounds on the trail, wouldn't it now? Ha ha ha!"

Dinner that night in the cabin was held in a subdued mood. Snooky and Maya did not feel much like eating, and even Bernard found that his appetite had been dampened by the day's events. Afterward they gathered around the fire, Bernard with Misty on his lap, her head curled against his shoulder like a baby's. The three of them sat in gloomy silence. Snooky tried to read, but after half an hour he threw the book down.

"I give up. There's nothing like a murder to spoil the simple rustic mood. I'm going to turn in early."

"Good idea," said his sister. "We will too."

As Bernard climbed into bed, he found his wife sitting up, a pensive expression on her face. "What is it?"

"I'm thinking about Snooky. Would you mind very much if we stayed on here for a while longer? I would feel awful leaving him in the middle of this murder investigation and everything."

"Not at all," said Bernard bitterly. "Why don't we sell our house and live here forever with Snooky? That would be a perfect solution."

"I'm glad you don't mind."

"Yes." Bernard rolled over onto his side and lay brooding in the pitch darkness. His vacation in Vermont had gone straight to hell. He was getting no work done at all, and people were getting shot to death outside his cabin. A sudden thought occurred to him. "Maya?" he whispered.

"Mmmhmmm?"

"Do you think that whoever killed him is still out there?"

"What?" she asked sleepily.

"You know. Out there—in the woods?"

"Oh, Bernard. Please."

"Waiting," breathed Bernard. His eyes grew round in the darkness. "Waiting . . . for another victim?"

"Bernard, please. I have to go to sleep."

"All right. Good night."

Maya rolled over and regarded the large bulk of her husband lovingly. "I'm sorry you had to be the one to find him, sweetheart. If you have bad dreams, wake me up, okay?"

"If I have bad dreams," said Bernard, pulling the covers up to his chin, "I'll be in the car and halfway home to Connecticut before I wake up myself."

Bernard woke up the next day relieved to find himself safe and sound in bed with the sun streaming in the windows. He had had disturbed dreams, visions of himself running in circles in the woods, nightmarish moments when Bobby Fuller's pale frozen visage floated in and out of his mind like a worm. He got out of bed, stretched, and shook himself all over.

Maya sat up and plumped the pillows behind her. "How did you sleep, sweetheart?"

"Badly."

"So did I."

At breakfast, Bernard made an interesting discovery, which was that an unexpected encounter with a frozen body the day before did not seem to have the power to affect his appetite this morning. He stuffed himself on eggs and bacon. Snooky, who ate very little at all times, barely touched the food. He sat back, sipping his coffee and watching Bernard with an awestruck look in his eyes.

"Look at him, Maya. Look at the man eat. Is he like that always, or is it the fresh air and exercise?"

"He's like that always."

"Is there any more coffee?" asked Bernard.

Snooky shook his head. "You shouldn't drink so much coffee and tea. It's bad for you, you know. It makes you jittery."

"Not me. It calms me down."

"Really? That's strange. That's very strange. What are your plans for today, My?"

"Don't you worry yourself about us, little one. We both have work to do."

"Another one of your articles?"

"Yes."

"What's this one on?"

"Siberian yurts."

Snooky brightened. "Yurts? Those tentlike things?"

"That's right."

"William would be so proud if he only knew. He always wanted us to grow up to write on things like Siberian yurts. At least one of us has managed to satisfy his ambitions."

"I don't know if William is really ever satisfied, no matter what we do."

"The trouble with William is, he can't relax. He spends his whole life in one huge spasm of tension. He never lets go. He's the most constipated personality I've ever met."

"Maybe one day he'll understand you, Snooks."

"Oh, yes. One day when he's about a million years old and his hair is gone and his eyes have fallen out and he can't hear anything, and he has to sit in a chair all day long and be waited on by unsympathetic nurses, that's when he'll understand me."

"That's right, Snooks. You'll be in the next chair."

"And you, Maya? Where will you be?"

"Bernard and me? We'll be in Tahiti, dancing to native rhythms."

Snooky smiled.

Later, as Snooky was leaving for Hugo's Folly, Bernard stopped him at the door. "Snooky," he whispered.

"Yes?"

"I want you to do something for me."

"Yes, Bernard?"

"I want you to find out what everyone in that family was doing yesterday afternoon. But be casual. Be very casual."

Snooky leaned against the doorjamb and crossed his arms in front of him. "I see. You want me to spy for you?"

"Spy is such a harsh word. Such a negative word. Just ask around. Be casual about it. Don't arouse any suspicions."

"I think this interest you have in the murder is a little macabre. Unhealthy, you know. I should speak to Maya about it."

"It would be interesting," said Bernard, "to know where everybody was. Don't you think so?"

"Well, that depends," said Snooky, taking his long red scarf and winding it around his neck several times. "It depends. If it wasn't really a hunting accident (and we know damn well it wasn't), and it turns out that everyone in the family was home crocheting in a big group by the fire, all except for Sarah, who happened to be standing over Bobby's body in the woods with a smoking gun, then, no, it wouldn't be terribly interesting. At least, not to me."

"So this is your camera," Snooky said half an hour later. "A Nikon, eh?"

"Yes," said Dwayne proudly. He caressed it lovingly.

"It's not the newest model, but it's one of the best. Takes beautiful pictures. I could show you some of my work, if you'd like."

"That would be terrific. So you were out taking photographs yesterday afternoon?"

"Yes. I spent most of the time following this bird around in the trees, trying to get a good shot of him against the sky. It wasn't easy. I like pictures of branches against the sky, don't you? Especially at this time of the year. The woods are so beautiful in the snow."

"So true," said Snooky, leaning back against the plush red velvet of the chair. They were seated in the living room of Hugo's Folly. "So very true. Did you happen to hear anything?"

"Hear anything?"

"Well . . . gunshots, for instance?"

"To tell you the truth, Snooky, I did hear something, but I didn't pay any attention. There are always hunters in the woods this time of year. None of them sounded very close, so I didn't look around. I never do. They're not going to shoot *me*, are they? Of course"—at this point he dropped his voice to a mournful moo—"that's what Bobby thought, isn't it?"

"Yes. Terrible," said Snooky lamely, thinking how insufficient most words were to describe the shock of sudden death. "Did you see anybody else while you were there?"

"Oh, no. Not a soul. I didn't hear anything, either, except some shots in the distance from time to time. I hope they didn't get a deer. I love deer, don't you? So elegant and beautiful." Dwayne's face took on a childlike expression. He fiddled absentmindedly with the camera shutter.

"I'm fond of deer myself."

"I've never eaten venison. Have you?"

"No."

"I don't think I could bring myself to touch it. Roger keeps telling me it's delicious, but fortunately there's not much chance of his bringing home a deer. He's not a very good shot."

"I had rabbit stew in France once," said Snooky.

"Really? Was it any good?"

"No."

"They eat dogs in Asia, so I've heard. I wonder if I should become a vegetarian," said Dwayne. He twisted around as the door opened. "Oh. Sarah. How's Aunt Irma?"

"Quiet," said Sarah, sitting down with them. "Very pale, very quiet. She's awake now, but she looks to me like she's still in shock. I wish she'd shout or scream or do something."

"She's still absorbing the news," said Snooky. "Has she eaten anything?"

"No."

"Can I fix her something?"

"Like what?"

"Oh, I don't know. I wish Bernard was here. He makes a hot toddy that puts you right out."

The two of them went into the kitchen, leaving Dwayne playing happily with his camera. Snooky gathered together some ingredients from the liquor cabinet and spices from the pantry, and mixed up a hot potion. "Here. Try that. I guarantee you it'll make her happier. It's an old family recipe. William used to make it in times of crisis. He never touches alcohol unless he can convince himself that it's medicinal."

Sarah gave him a quick kiss and went upstairs. Snooky went prowling for a new victim. He found Gertie standing in the laundry room, next to the kitchen, looking around her in a bewildered way.

"Now where did I leave my—ah!" she cried, pouncing on something on the floor. She held it up in triumph. It was, as far as Snooky could tell, a twig with a bit of moss attached to it.

"I suppose you don't recognize this?" she asked scornfully.

"Yes, as a matter of fact I do. It's a twig with a bit of moss on it."

Gertie snorted. She placed the specimen carefully in a

plastic bag and dropped it into one of the many voluminous pockets of her coat. "Anybody can tell you've never studied botany. Not like your sister, for instance."

"Oh, my sister is the shining intellectual light of the family. We've all known that for years. So you've been out in the woods?"

"Yes, I'm out every day. Just got back. I'll go out again this afternoon."

"Found anything recently?"

Gertie beamed. She rubbed her hands together and marched past him into the kitchen. She sat down at the counter and began to take off her green rubber boots. "Yesterday I saw a lizard," she said cheerfully. "Adorable. I'm not sure what type it was, it ran away too quickly. Delightful creature. And there were some lovely birds. Not much wildlife around these days, though. Everyone is holed up for the winter."

"You're dripping on the floor."

"So I am. Who cares? I always drip on the floor. A little mud never hurt anyone. Where was I? Oh, yes, yesterday was quite a day. I wish I could have gotten a better view of that lizard. It might have been an unusual type. The markings on it—"

"Did you run into Dwayne in the woods?"

"What's that? Dwayne? No." She let out a harsh hoot of laughter. "Dwayne and I have run into each other only once. Literally, I mean. He was pointing his camera at the sky, God only knows why, and I was following a chipmunk in the bushes. Neither of us was looking. I bumped into him and knocked him to the ground. Nearly broke his camera. He was nice enough about it, but I could tell he was upset."

"So you didn't see Dwayne. How about anyone else?"

A cautious look came into Gertie's mud-colored eyes. "Bobby Fuller, you mean? No, I didn't see him. I heard shots, but naturally you always hear shots in the woods this time of year. Whoever killed Bobby kept away from me. Which is just as well. The less I know about it, the better."

Snooky regarded her thoughtfully. "Really? Why is that?"

"Don't want to get involved," snapped Gertie, standing up and wiggling her toes luxuriously. "Don't want to know anything I shouldn't. I figure if there's some funny business going on in this family, the less I know, the safer I am."

"Well, that's true, of course."

"Glad you see it that way."

"Still, Gertie, you must admit that nobody's really upset about Bobby's death."

"We're not hypocrites, young man. We're an honest lot. My brother, Hugo, had bad taste—look at this house—but it was *honest* bad taste. Nobody here is wasting any time pretending. Bobby's death means a lot more money, some day, for all of us."

"Yes. I suppose that's true."

Gertie shot him a crafty look. "And if you'll take my advice, you'll stop poking around and asking so many questions about what happened. The less you know, the better."

It was a warning.

"Thank you. I'll keep that in mind, Gertie."

"You do that. Now I have to go catalog this specimen. Got to keep up to date on my journals." And she was gone, thumping through the house in her stocking feet. Snooky could hear her bedroom door slam shut overhead.

Snooky left the kitchen, his brow furrowed in thought, and made his way down the hall. He was standing in the foyer, gazing absently at the evil-eyed portraits on the walls, when the doorbell rang.

"Why, Detective Bentley. What an unexpected pleasure."

"I'm here to interview Irma Ditmar."

"I'm sorry, but I don't think that will be possible. She's not in very good shape. Her heart, remember. Why don't you arrange to come back tomorrow, or maybe next year?"

"I'll wait for her in the living room."

"No, you won't," said Sarah sharply, coming into the foyer. "As I told you yesterday, my aunt is in no shape to be harassed by the police. I've given her something to drink, and she's going back to sleep again. She's had a great shock to her system, and I'm not going to let anyone disturb her."

"All right," said Bentley, suddenly amicable. "While I'm here, Miss Tucker, where were you that afternoon?"

"That Bobby was killed? I've told you a hundred times, Detective. I was home all day. I made dinner for everyone."

"Everyone?"

"Gertie, Aunt Irma and myself."

"Can anyone corroborate where you were?"

Sarah looked at him frostily. "My aunt can, when she wakes up. You can see her tomorrow, but not before then."

"Thank you. By the way, Mr. Randolph, how about you?"

"Me?"

"Yes, you."

"Where was I when Bobby was killed?"

"Yes."

"I'm flattered to be considered a suspect, Detective. What exactly do you think my motive is?"

"Answer the question, please."

"Let me think. I was home in the cabin all day."

"Alone?"

"No. My sister was there. She can corroborate what I say."

"All right."

"Of course," Snooky said mildly, "I'm her favorite brother. She has a soft spot for me. She'd say anything I told her to. And my memory is so bad these days. Now let me think—was I home in the cabin, or was I out in the woods, hunting game with Roger's Winchester rifle?"

"Good-bye," Bentley said to Sarah. "I'll be here tomorrow morning around nine o'clock to interview Mrs. Ditmar."

"Good-bye, Detective."

"And as for you, young man," the detective said, "I'm glad you think it's so funny. Murder is no laughing matter."

Snooky, sobered, shut the door behind him. The little detective was right, he thought. *Murder is no laughing matter. . . .*

Bernard tapped absently on the typewriter keys as he listened to Snooky's report. "All right," he said. "So Dwayne and Gertie admit that they were in the woods, in the right spot at the right time. Roger and Sarah say they were home. Irma was home as well."

"Yes."

"Thank you, Snooky."

"Is that all, Bernard? Can I relax now? My spying duties are over for the moment?"

"Yes, thank you."

Snooky stood up, stretched like a cat and disappeared into his bedroom. Bernard looked at the page in the typewriter. His random typing spelled out:

MXCTLKEIC EKXLEKDJFIL C,EK3K4LSKCK05

His eyes took on a dreamy, faraway expression. He sat quietly for a few minutes, gazing at the hearth, then turned back to his typewriter.

GN?

This, in his own special shorthand, stood for "Gun?" Underneath he typed,

MTVE? (Motive?)
WLK N TH WDS ("walk in the woods")
NGGMNT ("engagement")
FMLY ("family")

He was looking in sleepy satisfaction at these notes when Snooky came back in and settled down on the sofa with a book.

"You don't mind if I read in here, do you? It's too cold in my bedroom. Where's that blanket? By the way, Bernard, I've decided we're having chicken à l'orange tonight. How's that?"

"Fine."

"I'll go shopping a little later on." Snooky leaned back on the cushions with a sigh. "It's good to be young, and have nothing to do. You don't understand that, do you, Bernard? Were you ever young?"

"I was young," Bernard said shortly.

"I can't imagine it. I can't see it, personally. It's not something I can picture. You, young." Snooky put his head on one side. "Nope, I can't visualize it."

"I was young. I was your age once. I was your age only seven years ago."

"What was it like for you then? You hadn't met Maya yet, had you? What was it like?"

"It was," said Bernard, "a barren wasteland."

"Because you hadn't met my sister?"

"Yes."

"That's touching, Bernard. A little nauseating, but touching. Where were you living then?"

"In New York City."

"Really? Where?"

"On the Upper West Side. I had a studio apartment. It

was the size of this living room. Maybe a little smaller. The bathroom was in the kitchen."

"Sounds luxurious. Were you dating?"

"Now and then," Bernard said stiffly.

"Really? Who?"

"None of your business, Snooky."

"Oh, come on. It's just the two of us. Maya isn't around. What kind of women were you dating? What were they like?"

"They were morons and imbeciles, with an occasional psychotic thrown in."

Snooky nodded. "I can understand that. I really can. That's what it looks like, sometimes. Like you're the only sane person and the rest of the world is crazy."

"Yes."

"And then you met Maya."

"Yes. At a party. A literary party."

"No. You? You went to a *party?*"

"I was forced to go."

"By whom?"

"My agent."

"Oh. So you met Maya there."

"Yes."

"And you asked her out?"

"Yes, I did."

Snooky waited, but Bernard was not forthcoming. He had lapsed into a melancholy silence.

"You know," said Snooky, "I don't want to complain, because you and I so rarely have these little tête-à-têtes, but I've talked to dogs that were more communicative."

"It's a simple enough story, Snooky. You know most of it. I dated before I met your sister. Then I met her. Then we got married. Then I found out about you. You know the kind of hell that's turned my life into."

"When you met Maya, did you have a special feeling?" asked Snooky tentatively. "You know . . . a special feeling?"

"A special feeling. Yes. Yes, I did." Bernard drummed his fingers on the top of his typewriter.

"What did it feel like?"

"I don't know, Snooky," Bernard said irritably. "I can't describe it."

"Was it different from anything you had ever felt before?"

"Yes, it was."

"How soon did you know you were going to marry her?"

"I don't really know. After a few months, maybe. It takes me a while to get to know someone. By the way, is this conversation about Maya and me, or is it about you and your numerous girlfriends?"

"I've never had a special feeling," said Snooky sadly. "Never."

Bernard stared at him gloomily, signifying that he did not particularly care. Misty stirred and yawned. They could hear Maya humming in the kitchen as she prepared lunch. The cold blue sunlight slanted in through the windows and gleamed chestnut-gold on Snooky's hair.

"So what were they like?"

"Who?"

"These women that you dated."

"I've already told you. Morons, psychotics and imbeciles."

"What else?"

Bernard bared his teeth at him. "I don't like to talk about my old girlfriends when Maya is around."

"Why? She doesn't care."

"I know, but it upsets me, and then she has to calm me down. Well, when I first came to New York, I met a woman who worked in advertising. She was crazy. All she ever did was work and smoke. She never ate. We didn't have much in common."

"Uh-huh. I can see that. And then?"

"Then I went out with a woman who worked in real estate. She had a little brat of about five or six who hated me. That didn't last long."

"The kid hated you?"

"Yes."

"How could that be?"

"Don't be coy, Snooky. You know how much I hate children. Well, this little kid hated me back. He used to pinch me when his mother wasn't looking."

"Did you tell on him?"

"No."

"Oh. I would have. And then?"

"Well, there was one other person I dated in New York before I met Maya. She worked at the Metropolitan Museum of Art. She was a curator or something, I never got it straight. We used to go to concerts there together. She was a good person." Bernard seemed to sink further into a melancholy mood.

"What happened?"

"She left me. Suddenly. Her old boyfriend came back to town and she went back to him."

Snooky was thunderstruck. "I've been left. I know how that feels. Were you upset?"

"No," said Bernard. "I was delighted. Naturally I was upset. What do you think, Snooky? Do you think I have no feelings at all?"

"Were you on the rebound when you met my sister?"

"No. That was almost a year later."

"Tell me, Bernard. If this woman dumped you—"

"I wouldn't say 'dumped,'" objected Bernard. " 'Dumped' is such a cruel, unfeeling word. I would say 'betrayed.' "

"Whatever. If this woman left you, does that make her a moron, a psychotic or an imbecile?"

Bernard brightened perceptibly. "I hadn't thought of that."

"Perhaps all three," said Snooky kindly, and settled back on the couch with his book.

Later that evening, Snooky cornered Maya in the kitchen. He said in an excited whisper, "Bernard and I had a conversation this afternoon, Maya. An entire conversation. We sat and talked in the living room, just the two of us."

"I'm so happy for you that I could cry." Maya was heating up some milk for cocoa. "What do you think? Is this hot enough?"

"Wait till it bubbles around the edges. We sat and we talked for a long time. Bernard opened up and told me more about his past than he ever has before. Maybe more than he's ever told anyone before, except of course for you."

"I'm sure that made his day." She measured plain baking cocoa and sugar into three mugs.

"I don't see why you have to be so cynical. Bernard and I have never had a real conversation before."

"Bernard told me about it, too," said Maya, tilting the hot milk from the pan into the mugs.

"Did he? Did he really? What did he say? Was he excited about it, too?"

"Yes, he was, Snooky."

"I knew it. It was a breakthrough in our relationship, Maya. A breakthrough. What did he say to you?"

"Well, you know Bernard. He doesn't say much."

"Yes, I know. But he must have said something about it."

"Well, if you really want to know, he said, 'Snooky was prying into my past today. I told him about Diane.'"

Snooky was crestfallen. "Diane? Is that the art museum curator?"

"Yes."

"That's it? That's all he said?"

"I'm afraid so."

"That I was *prying into his past?*"

"Yes."

"It's so unfair. I don't understand it. How can you get along with him?"

"He did say one more thing."

"Really? What was that?"

"He asked if I could manage to keep you out of the living room while he's trying to work from now on."

Snooky was furious. "This is the end. I've had it. My trust and confidence have been abused once too often. And to think that I spied on my own girlfriend's family for him. How can you have married him, Maya? The man has no human attributes whatsoever."

"Don't fret, little one," she said affectionately, and handed him a cup of cocoa.

The next morning at nine o'clock, Snooky was at the door of Hugo's Folly to greet Detective Bentley.

"Detective. What a pleasure. I could hardly sleep all night, knowing that you'd be here today."

"Is Mrs. Ditmar ready?"

"She'll be down in a minute. Come with me." Snooky led the way into the living room, where he and the detective sat and stared at each other.

"It's a strange business," Snooky said at last. "Any idea who did it?"

"We're following up on every clue we have, Mr. Randolph."

"Yes. Yes, I'm sure you are."

The door opened and Irma came in, leaning on Sarah's arm. She was very pale today and wore no makeup at all. In the harsh silver light of the living room, she looked nearly a hundred years old. She was wearing a peach-colored satin bathrobe over a nightgown, and on her feet were fuzzy bunny slippers. The contrast of her blue-veined legs and the childish slippers was strangely incongruous, and touching. Irma sank into one of the armchairs with a grateful sigh.

"Mrs. Ditmar," said Bentley. "Thank you for seeing me."

"You're welcome."

"I understand what a shock this must have been."

"Yes," Irma said simply. The skin around her mouth whitened, her lips drawing inward.

"Mrs. Ditmar, please tell me about your relationship with Bobby Fuller."

"We were engaged to be married."

"And you announced your engagement—?"

"Last Friday. A few days before he died."

"How long had you known him?"

"About three months."

"Would you say the news of your engagement came as a shock to your family?"

"They were delighted," said Irma firmly. "Absolutely delighted. Anyone who knew Bobby would be."

"Where were you on the day he died?"

"I was here, in the house."

"Alone?"

"No, Sarah was with me."

"All day?"

Irma looked at her niece appealingly. "Well, of course we weren't together every *minute* of the day . . ."

"My aunt was upstairs and I was downstairs, in the kitchen," said Sarah smoothly.

"But you were both in the house all day?"

"Well, of course I *did* go out for a little while to do the shopping . . ." said Irma.

"And you were here alone?" said Bentley to Sarah.

"Yes, Detective. But I stayed right here. I was busy making pot roast in the kitchen. It was a new recipe and everything always takes so much longer when you do it for the first time."

"So true," piped up Snooky. "I remember once, I was trying out this new recipe for mushroom strudel, and it took me forever. You wouldn't think it could be so difficult, but it can. I couldn't get the pastry to fold up right, and—"

"When was the last time you saw Bobby Fuller?" Bentley asked Irma.

"—Kept ten people waiting for dinner," Snooky concluded, unruffled. "Finally had to send out for pizza."

"Oh, I don't know," said Irma. "Let me see. Oh, yes, it was Saturday. The day after Snooky's dinner party. We went out for dinner and a movie. That was the last time."

"Mrs. Ditmar, who would want to kill your fiancé?"

Irma met his gaze calmly. "Nobody."

"Nobody?"

"Absolutely not. Everyone loved Bobby. They were happy for me, because I was happy. So very happy. And let me tell you, Detective, that any suspicions you might have about my family are simply—well, simply ridiculous. I resent it."

"So what is your explanation of your fiancé's death?"

Irma produced a lacy white handkerchief from the pocket of her bathrobe and waved it vaguely in the air. "An accident," she said. "A tragic, tragic accident. That's what it was."

The detective took her over and over this, but Irma held fast to her belief that Bobby had died as the result of a hunting accident. "It *does* happen. You remember, there was that case in New Hampshire last winter. Those hunters are crazy. They'll shoot at anything."

"Does that include your brother?"

Irma stiffened. A steely glint came into her seawater-green eyes. Her eyes looked paler than usual, washed out, as if all the tears had drained them of their normal color. "Roger is different," she said fiercely. "Roger is a . . . a *humanist.*"

Nobody knew what she meant by this, but she said it proudly, as a mark of esteem. Bentley was puzzled. "You don't think he would shoot at anything that moved out there?"

"No, no, of course not. If he had a trigger finger, he'd have shot Gertie long ago. She's always taking her nature walks while he's out hunting in the same section of the woods."

Snooky felt she had a point. Gertie was so large that while it seemed impossible that she could be mistaken for a deer—a moose, perhaps, or a caribou, although he didn't think they inhabited these parts—there was no doubt that she afforded a neat target. If Gertie had spent years marching in safety through the woods, that argued against the hunting accident theory.

"That's insulting," Irma was saying now, her voice raised. "That's insulting, Detective."

Bentley was looking slightly cowed. "It's something I have to ask you, Mrs. Ditmar."

"How dare you imply that anyone in my family—*my family*—would kill anyone for money! As if I would cut them off without a cent anyway! They know me better than that. I wouldn't have left all my money to Bobby—why, it wouldn't have been *fair!*"

Sarah, Snooky noticed, was gazing out the window with a peculiar expression on her face.

"It was Hugo's money, anyway. I owe it to him to take care of the family. I've always been fair about the money, everyone knows that. So it's ridiculous to imply that anybody thought I'd let Bobby steal the money away from them. Money is a great responsibility," said Irma heatedly. "A truly great responsibility. That's why Hugo left it all to me. He knew I had a business sense, that I could handle it. And I won't listen to any more lies and slander. Everyone wishes me well; everyone in the family loves me. Do you have a family, Detective?"

Bentley, who was in fact an orphan and a bachelor, shook his head.

"I knew it," Irma said cunningly. "No family, eh? Well, then you don't understand. You don't know what it's like. But I won't listen to any more of these innuendos. Sarah, come with me."

Bristling with indignation, she rose to her feet and left the room. Snooky and the little detective sat in silence for a moment.

"She knows something," Bentley said at last, "but she's not telling."

"This is a family, Detective. They all stick together."

Bentley shook his head. As an orphan and a bachelor, he had spent his life on the outside of families, looking in. Irma's discovery of this had bruised his feelings. He had a tender inner core on the subject, like a lonely barnacle. Now he shook his head again. "Families!"

"They'll do anything to protect each other."

"Even hide a murderer in their midst?"

"Yes," said Snooky slowly. "I think so. Even hide a murderer."

Bernard looked up from his typewriter as Snooky came in. "Hi. How was the interview?"

"Honestly, Bernard," said Snooky, dumping a bag full of groceries onto the table, "I don't see how you can ask that. Don't you know that I hate people prying into my past? Yes, I sat in on the interview, and yes, I know all about it, and no, I'm not going to tell you a word. I respect your privacy, you respect mine." He went into his bedroom and the door shut with a bang.

Bernard was puzzled. "What's the matter with him?"

"He's a little ticked off about that talk you had yesterday," said Maya.

"The talk?"

"What you said about it afterward. He didn't feel you appreciated it very much."

"Oh." Bernard thrummed absently on the typewriter keys. "I hope this doesn't mean I have to apologize. I hate to apologize."

"I know you do."

"I've never had to apologize to Snooky. It doesn't seem fair, does it? It's not like I did anything wrong."

Maya pursed her lips and went back to her book. Bernard sat typing "shit shit shit shit shit" over and over. Finally, with a sigh, he heaved himself out of the chair. "We are his guests."

"Yes."

"I guess I have to be polite."

Bernard stood in front of Snooky's bedroom door for a few minutes, wrestling over what he should say. Finally he raised his voice. "Snooky?"

There was no answer.

"Snooky, you shouldn't be so sensitive. You'll get your feelings hurt all the time. It's not right."

There was silence.

"That's excellent, darling," said Maya encouragingly. "First hurt his feelings, then attack him for being too sensitive."

"Snooky, I'm sorry I hurt your feelings. I did enjoy our little chat yesterday. It made my day. It was the single most profoundly moving discussion I've ever had with anyone in my life."

Silence behind the door.

"Snooky, I've done what I can. I've apologized, and that's enough. I'm going back to my seat now. You're acting childish, in my opinion. You can come out whenever you want to. I'm not going to beg. There are limits to everything."

"That was a good apology," said Maya, turning a page. "You did say somewhere in there, when you weren't yelling at him, that you were sorry?"

"Uh-huh."

"Well, that's enough. It's up to him now."

The silence continued behind the door for the next hour, at the end of which Snooky appeared sleepy-eyed and yawning, his hair tousled over his forehead. "What time is it?"

Maya glanced at her watch. "Nearly twelve-thirty."

"Eeks. It's time for lunch. Maya, will you give me a hand?"

"First I think you should say something to Bernard," Maya said pointedly. She gestured with her book. "He's been waiting out here for an hour."

"Waiting? For what?"

"For you to respond to what he said."

"I'm sorry, My. I'm not following you. What did he say?"

"Come on, Snooky. He stood outside your door and apologized very nicely for what happened yesterday."

Snooky smiled. "Did he? Did you, Bernard? That's kind of you. That's really nice. You have a good heart, Bernard. That's what I've always said about you in case anyone asked, did you know that? You have a good heart. That's what your name means, you know, 'bear's heart.' Brave and stalwart as a bear."

Bernard was scrubbing at a page with an eraser shaped like a bunny rabbit.

"I was sleeping," Snooky said to Maya. "I was so tired when I got home that I took a nap. You know I can never be angry at anyone for long. Remember that time William killed my turtle by accident? I was talking to him again within the year. I have a forgiving nature, Maya. You know that."

"Yes, I do, Snookers."

"Of course," said Snooky, a sly expression stealing over his face, "since I slept right through Bernard's magnificent apology, perhaps he wouldn't mind repeating it? Just for me. Now that I'm awake."

Sullenly, Bernard repeated it. "I said I was sorry."

Snooky looked let down. "That's all?"

"I said I was sorry for hurting your feelings."

"That's nice, Bernard. That's it?"

"Yes." At a glance from Maya, Bernard continued grudgingly, "I said I enjoyed our little talk yesterday."

"He said it was the most profound conversation he's ever had," supplied Maya.

"It was. I feel like a different person. Now can I get back to work?"

"Of course you can," said Snooky. "Was that it? That was the apology?"

"It was a good apology," said Bernard stiffly. "It was a fine apology."

"Nothing more abject than that?"

"No."

"Oh. Well, I'm sorry I missed it. It sounds like a once-in-a-lifetime experience. My, will you help me with lunch?"

"Okay."

In the kitchen, Maya said disapprovingly, "You weren't asleep, were you?"

"No, of course I wasn't."

"You heard everything he said?"

"Every last word."

"And you just wanted to hear it over again?"

"I can't help it, My." Snooky unloaded the groceries onto the counter and began to sort through the vegetables. "I figured it was an unprecedented opportunity to have a once-in-a-lifetime experience twice in one day."

"I see," Bernard said later. Snooky was filling him in on the police interview with Irma. While he listened, Bernard aimlessly typed *Mrs. Woolly is a jerk* over and over again on the page. "So she was out of the house for part of the time that day?"

"Yes."

"I see." *Mrs. Woolly is a jerk Mrs. Woolly is a jerk.* "So she could have driven out to the woods and killed her fiancé herself."

Snooky looked disgusted. He was stretched out on the sofa, one hand absently rubbing Misty's head, the other hand supporting a cup of hot coffee on his stomach. Misty was splayed out on the floor in a position of ecstasy. "Yes, Bernard. Oh, yes. That would make a lot of sense."

"All right. So your friend Sarah doesn't have an alibi for the entire afternoon, either."

"That's right." Snooky looked faintly despondent. He scratched Misty's head thoughtfully. Misty made a low rumbling, scratchy, hiccuping sound. "Do you hear these sounds Misty's making? I think she's trying to purr. Are you sure she knows she's a dog?"

"Do you think your friend is telling the truth?"

"Sarah? Yes, I do. I don't think she left the house, and I know she didn't kill Bobby."

"How do you know?"

Snooky shrugged. "How can you say whether or not somebody is a murderer? I don't think she's capable of that. No matter how angry she was, or how much she wanted her aunt's money, I can't see her stealing that gun and pulling the trigger."

"Thank you for that character analysis, Snooky. We all know how accurate your readings of the women you date are."

"I still don't think she would have done it."

"I wonder who did," mused Bernard. *Mrs. Woolly is a jerk Mrs. Woolly is a jerk Mrs. Woolly is a jerk.*

"What about Roger? It was his gun, after all."

"That brings us back to the same question. If you're going to kill somebody, is it smart or stupid to use your own gun?"

"In this case, it doesn't seem to matter. Detective Bentley wouldn't know who it was if they had written their name in blood in the snow nearby."

"You underestimate him. I think in that case he would know."

"Well, it doesn't matter." Some coffee slurped out onto Snooky's shirt and he gave a muffled yelp. "What about Gertie? She was in the woods that day, too."

Gertie is a jerk Gertie is a jerk Gertie is a jerk, typed Bernard absently. "Maybe."

"That's all? Just, 'maybe'?"

"I don't know, Snooky. If she had done it, wouldn't she have made some effort to have an alibi?"

"I guess so." Snooky rubbed at the coffee spot on his shirt. "How do you get coffee out? Is it soap and water, or lemon, or baking soda, or what?"

"I don't know. Ask Maya."

"All right. How about Dwayne? I agree he seems a little dim to have planned this, but it's a straightforward kind of murder. He says he's going out with his camera, takes Roger's gun out of the closet—he would know where it's kept, he lives there, for God's sake—goes out into the woods, finds Bobby and blows his brains out. He leaves the gun in the woods to implicate Roger, then comes home and pretends that nothing has happened. It would be easy for him."

Dwayne is a jerk Dwayne is a jerk Dwayne is a jerk, typed Bernard. He was lost in thought. "It's possible. Whoever left the gun there definitely wanted to get Roger into trouble. Could there be somebody else? How about somebody outside the family?"

"Outside the family? A neighbor, you mean? What would their motive be?"

"I don't know. There's so much I don't know," Bernard said humbly. *Mrs. Woolly is a jerk Mrs. Woolly is a jerk Mrs. Woolly is a jerk.*

"Well, there's one thing I do know," said Snooky. He tipped his long legs over the side of the couch and stood up, stretching. "If I don't put this shirt in hot water or lemon juice or baking powder or something, this spot will never come out."

Detective Bentley came out of the Grunwald sisters' house and strode manfully down the walkway, his short legs pumping like pistons. He got into his old yellow car, which after some preliminary reluctance came to life and moved jerkily away down the village street.

Alicia and Charlotte Grunwald stood at the window of their house. Finally Alicia said firmly, "What an *awful* man."

"Awful!" echoed Charlotte.

"He's too short to be so arrogant, don't you think?"

"Oh, yes."

"Of course it's always the short men who are the worst," said Alicia shrewdly. This was based on absolutely no knowledge of the opposite sex whatsoever.

"Yes, yes, that's so true, Alicia."

"Think of Napoleon."

"Oh, yes."

"He probably has some kind of complex about it."

"Some kind of complex," echoed Charlotte. "More tea?"

"Thank you, dear."

Tea was poured out, and milk and sugar distributed generously. Alicia stood at the window, her eyes on the empty street.

"Lishie . . . ," faltered Charlotte.

"Yes, Lotty?" They never used their pet names in front of anybody else; it was too private and, in Alicia's opinion, the names were too silly.

"Lishie, do you think we should have told him?"

Alicia sipped her tea absently, her eyes still on the street, where now nothing moved. Traffic did not often come through Lyle; it was far away from the usual tourist thoroughfares.

"No." She put her teacup down on the saucer with a firm *clink*. "Why should we tell him, that terrible man? Let him find out for himself, if he can. We found out by ourselves, didn't we?"

"Oh, yes . . . yes, we certainly did."

"It would kill Irma if she knew," Alicia said with grim cheerfulness. "She'd have a heart attack, poor dear. That reminds me, Lotty. We still have to pay our condolence call."

"Condolence call. Yes . . ."

"Poor Irma. Poor dear Irma."

"Poor Irma . . ."

"Perhaps we could drop by tomorrow morning, and still be back here in time for lunch."

"Tomorrow morning . . ."

"Yes, that's what we'll do. And I'll go by the florist's bright and early and pick up some nice flowers. Poor dear Irma!"

The next morning Snooky was at the Ditmar mansion again. He had become a sort of unofficial butler to the house. Sarah was busy upstairs with her aunt, and Gertie was (as always) out in the woods frightening the wildlife. When the doorbell rang, Snooky answered it.

Two tall, painfully thin, gray-faced old ladies confronted him on the doorstep.

"Hello," said one of them, shouldering her way forward

with authority. She carried a small bunch of chrysanthemums and roses. "Is Irma here? We wanted to pay our respects."

"You're the Grunwalds, aren't you?"

"Yes. I'm Alicia."

"Charlotte," faltered the other one, pronouncing her name like an apology.

"I think we've met briefly before. I'm Sarah's boyfriend Snooky Randolph. You remember—in the market a few weeks ago . . . ?"

"Oh, yes," said Alicia. "Is Irma in?"

"She's upstairs. I'm afraid she's not feeling too well. Why don't you let me tell her that you're here?"

"Thank you, that would be kind."

"Please come into the living room."

Snooky saw them safely settled in the living room, then went upstairs. He came down a few minutes later with Irma on his arm and Sarah trailing after them. "I'm going to come in with you," Sarah had told him. "I don't trust those two old bats. I don't want them upsetting Aunt Irma."

"All right."

Irma clasped her hands together in delight at the sight of her two old friends. "Charlotte . . . Alicia . . . how kind of you to come."

The three old women kissed awkwardly. The flowers were presented, and Irma took them with what seemed to Snooky exaggerated cries of delight. "Thank you . . . so beautiful . . . very kind of you." He helped Irma settle down on a green-and-white striped divan, and he and Sarah sat nearby. The three ladies faced each other. There was a long, agonizing pause.

Finally Alicia broke the silence.

"Irma, my dear, it's so awful. We feel for you so much. What a loss . . . a tragic loss."

"Tragic loss," murmured Charlotte.

Irma lifted her chin proudly. "Thank you. So kind of you. Yes, you're right. It is a great loss to me."

"He was a fine young man."

"Yes, he was."

"And how are you doing, dear Irma?"

Irma sighed and one hand went tragically to her face. "Not very well, I'm afraid. Not well at all. My heart, you know. It's never been strong."

The two Grunwalds murmured a sympathetic reply, buzzing together like a large kindly bee.

It occurred to Snooky that what he was seeing was a stage set, a scene being enacted for the benefit of the principal actors concerned. The Grunwalds were not really unhappy that Bobby was dead, and Irma was not overcome with joy at having to welcome them into her home. But all three were determined to play the scene through. The Grunwalds could then go home satisfied that they had done their duty, and Irma could take to her bed again, satisfied that she had upheld the family dignity. While musing on this, he missed a few questions and replies.

When he began to pay attention again, Charlotte was saying in her timid way, "But, Irma . . . it must be so difficult for you . . . how are you managing here alone?"

"I'm not alone," Irma said proudly. "I have my family." She turned to Sarah with a smile, and was greeted by an affectionate one in return.

"Yes . . . yes, Sarah, of course . . . and Gertie."

"Yes."

"And Dwayne?" asked Alicia in her deep voice. "Is he here, or is he off gallivanting? We live next door, but we see him so rarely these days."

Irma stiffened. "Dwayne has been wonderful—simply wonderful. And Roger. They've all been so kind to me. As you would be to each other," she added cannily, "if one of you had such a great loss."

There was a pause while the Grunwald sisters reflected on the fact that neither of them had ever had a lover, and therefore no opportunity for such a loss. Charlotte sat up straighter and said, "You know . . . you must think that you truly are *lucky* . . . to have had the affection you shared."

"Oh, yes, Charlotte. Yes, I do feel that, and it comforts me. At least we had that time together. Except for the early years with Hugo, it was the most special time of my life."

Alicia and Charlotte, sensing somehow that their time was up, chattered on about trivialities for a short while longer and then rose to their feet as one. "Dear Irma," said Alicia, bending down to give her a sisterly kiss. "So good to see you. Promise you'll drop by when you're feeling better."

"Thank you, Alicia."

"Irma . . . ," murmured Charlotte, giving her a peck on the cheek. "So good to see you."

"Charlotte. Kind of you to come. Thank you again for the lovely flowers."

There was much fluttering and scarf arranging and shrugging on of coats and mufflers at the front door. Alicia settled her gray woolly cap onto her gray woolly curls. Charlotte put on an identical cap and they marched off down the driveway. Snooky closed the door behind them.

Irma came out into the foyer and tossed the bouquet of flowers onto the umbrella stand with a disdainful gesture. "Cheap," she announced. "Cheap. Eighteen dollars and thirty-five cents at Mercer's Flower Shop. The cheapest one they have. Those two old vipers! Can you help me up to bed, dear? I feel absolutely exhausted from the effort of seeing them."

While Alicia Grunwald, marching down the driveway, turned at the same moment to her sister and said with spiteful satisfaction,

"That old bat. That old bat! If only she knew the truth . . . the most special time of her life, indeed! If she only *knew!*"

5

Snooky was at Harry's Market a few days later, picking out lettuce and tomatoes and cucumber for a salad, when a shy tug on his elbow made him look up.

It was Charlotte Grunwald, her gray cap jammed firmly on her head, her hands encased in woollen gloves. She smiled at him shyly. "Hello."

"Hello, Charlotte. Nice seeing you. How are you?"

"Fine, thank you."

"Is your sister here, too?"

"Oh, no, Alicia rarely does the shopping. I do most of the shopping and cooking for both of us. It works out better that way. Alicia's so *busy*, you see," she added in a flustered way, as if aware of a subtle reproach in her own words. "She has her work, you know."

"Her work?"

"Oh, yes . . . yes. She's an historian, you see. It's what she trained for. She's . . . she's quite avid about it. Reads all the time. I can't understand a word of it myself."

"I see."

"Her specialty is prerevolutionary New England. She's

deep into a biography right now of John and Abigail Adams. I think it's terribly boring myself, but then, she always tells me I don't have a brain in my head." Charlotte picked happily over the tomatoes.

"I'm sure that's not true!"

"Oh, well, it is true, I'm afraid. Alicia has all the brains in the family. She has enough for two."

Snooky did not say what he thought, which was that Alicia Grunwald's avocation struck him as a perfect excuse to stay home and read historical romances while her unfortunate younger sister did all the work running the house. "Nice tomatoes today, aren't they?"

"Very nice. Harry always carries the best. That's why I shop here."

Snooky flailed about for something to say. "It was nice of the two of you to come by and see Irma," he said at last, hating himself for his duplicity.

"Oh . . . well, it's such a *tragedy*. We felt so awful . . . we had to do something."

"Yes. It's hard to know what to do at a time like that, isn't it?"

"Very hard . . ."

"Hard to know what to say to her."

"Hard to know . . ."

"But I think the gesture is what counts, don't you?"

"Oh, yes . . . the gesture . . ."

Snooky began to feel unpleasantly that unless he took matters firmly in hand, the conversation would consist entirely of statements and echoes. But Charlotte surprised him by picking up a tomato, examining it warily, placing it in her basket and continuing in her soft voice, "Of course, naturally I shouldn't say anything . . . it's not kind to speak badly of the dead . . . but I don't really think . . . that is, Alicia and I don't really think . . . that everything was just the way poor dear Irma and her family thought it was."

Snooky leaned his shopping basket against the produce stand. "That's interesting. What makes you say that?"

"Oh, *well*," said Charlotte, picking through the lettuce eagerly. She was enjoying this chance to talk to a young man, to be away from her sister and out from under her dominating influence. Her personality expanded erratically in all directions, like a carnival balloon, all globes and cylinders and long jolly tubes. She leaned toward him in a giggly, confiding manner. "Oh, well, you see . . . Bobby was . . . oh, I probably shouldn't say a *word* . . . I'm sure Alicia wouldn't like it if . . . oh, well. I don't think my sister would approve, but I'm sure you wouldn't . . . if you know what I mean . . . oh, it's awful to speak ill of those who have passed on, especially so . . . so *violently*, isn't it?" She shuddered delicately and pawed at the cucumbers.

Snooky was not sure what she had said in this incoherent little speech, but he nodded knowingly. She leaned toward him again and gazed around the store, a happy expression in her granite-gray eyes. Her cap, under closer inspection, appeared to be made up of a multitude of tiny steel wool pads. "Well, it turns out . . . we saw something, Alicia and I. We know something about him . . ."

"Bobby?"

"Yes . . . he wasn't what he seemed to be, no, no, not at all. He was . . . well, he was . . . a *fraud*."

"A fraud?" Snooky thought how ironic life was, that he was now the faithful echo to Charlotte's conversation.

"Yes! All the time he was dancing around Irma, all that time, he was . . . he was *lying* to her." She leaned closer to him, her hat scratching unpleasantly against his cheek. *"He was seeing somebody else,"* she breathed, and gave him a triumphant look.

Snooky said the first thing that came into his head. "Why, Charlotte, that's . . . that's *amazing*."

She expanded visibly, her confidence billowing out into the wide aisles of the store, wedging itself between the bibb lettuce and the grapes. She clucked and preened herself fondly, like a little gray bird. "Isn't it?"

"Are you sure?"

"Oh, yes, yes . . . you see, we actually saw them to-

94

gether . . . Bobby and this—this hussy . . . all blond and made up . . ." She let her voice trail off disdainfully. "Good-looking blonde, but no *class*, if you know what I mean."

"You saw them here, in town?"

"Oh, no, Bobby would never be seen with her here. Too many wagging tongues about, if you know what I mean." Charlotte glanced around, apparently unaware of what her own tongue was busy doing at that moment. "We saw them in Wolfingham one day. Alicia and I were doing some shopping, and I couldn't find the right color wool here in Lyle for a sweater I was knitting for my godson's new baby . . . the cutest little thing you ever saw . . . the baby, I mean. He weighed nearly nine pounds at birth and his poor mother was in labor for thirty hours, it's so awful, isn't it? We women have *so* much to bear."

"How true," murmured Snooky.

"His name is Matthew Robert, and he's the sweetest little thing, truly he is," Charlotte said ecstatically. "But anyway . . . where was I? Oh, yes. I wanted to knit him a little winter sweater in sky blue and white, and Frasier's didn't have the right color blue"—this was the all-purpose store in town—"I wanted something a little bit *special*, you know, for Matthew, a true robin's-egg blue. So Alicia and I went into Wolfingham, which we rarely do these days, just when we need something special. They have a beautiful knitting store there, the most gorgeous wool, I've never seen anything like it, I really should speak to Frasier's about it, it's a scandal, you know, the cheap stuff they carry." She paused, giving him a buoyant smile. "Anyway—oh, I *am* enjoying this conversation, I hope I'm not boring you—anyway, we were coming out of the knitting store there, but we weren't quite out of the door, so he couldn't see us, and there was Bobby, walking down the street with his arm around this blond woman. And they were . . . well, the only decent way to describe it was that they were making eyes at each other. Pawing each other, really. It was enough to make your skin crawl. Especially when you think how devoted he always pretended to be toward poor Irma, and how she wanted to marry him and give him all her money and everything. Naturally that was what Alicia and I thought later, that he was with her for the money. A gold digger. Anyway, they didn't see us—of course they wouldn't have seen us even if we had been standing on the street in front of them, they had eyes only for each other—and we watched them go by, and then we went on our way. Isn't that *frightful!*" She pronounced the last word with relish.

"Yes. Frightful is the very word. But how clever of the two of you to have seen it, and not to be seen yourselves."

"Yes. Wasn't it? I'm sure he had no idea—no idea at all that his little secret was out."

"When was this?"

"Oh, I don't know. About a month ago."

Snooky calculated rapidly in his head. "A few weeks before Bobby was killed?"

"Yes, I suppose so."

"Before he and Irma announced their engagement?"

"Oh, yes, I'm quite sure it was."

Snooky deliberately gave her an admiring glance. "You've been very clever, Charlotte."

Charlotte licked her lips and nearly began to purr. "Do you really think so?"

"Absolutely. So you have no idea who the woman was?"

"None at all. A hussy, that's how Alicia refers to her. A brazen hussy."

"I see. The worst kind of hussy," remarked Snooky. "A brazen one. And have you told Detective Bentley about what you saw?"

Charlotte shook her head scornfully. "We were going to tell the police, because we knew it might be important, but when that awful little man came to our house it was all so unpleasant that we decided not to say anything. Anyway, Alicia decided not to. I sort of wondered to myself . . . perhaps we should have said *something*. It doesn't seem right that nobody would know."

"Well, your secret is safe with me."

Charlotte looked at him gratefully. "Thank you. And I should be going now. Alicia will be wondering what's happened to me. It's an amazing story, though, isn't it? I've been just . . . well, simply *bursting* to tell somebody. I feel ever so much better now. Relieved. It was kind of you to listen. You won't tell anyone?"

"No, no, of course not."

"It would be terrible if Irma found out," Charlotte said. "That's partly why Alicia and I decided not to tell. I think the news would kill her. After all, she was planning to *marry* the man. You won't tell anyone about it? Especially her family?"

"I promise."

Charlotte nodded. "So very nice talking to you," she said, her voice floating back over the piles of vegetables and fruit. "See you around, I hope."

"See you."

Snooky waited until she was out of the store, then grabbed his groceries, paid for them and sprinted for his car.

". . . and then they saw Bobby and some woman coming down the street hand in hand," he was telling Bernard a quarter of an hour later. "Down the street hand in hand. In full view. In her words, they were 'making eyes at each other.' "

Bernard appeared to be sunken in thought. His eyelids flickered.

"I wonder if anybody else knew about this." Snooky gnawed at a fingernail worriedly. "Maybe there was no reason to kill him. Maybe he wasn't planning to go through with the marriage after all."

Bernard stirred on the sofa. "Or maybe he *was* planning to go through with it, and this mystery woman is the one who killed him."

Snooky was struck by this. "True."

"We have to find out who she is."

"Yes."

"How do we do that?" mused Bernard. His eyes flickered aimlessly around the room, coming to rest at last on the languid figure of his brother-in-law. "You have to find out who she is, Snooky."

"Me? Why me? How am I supposed to find her?"

"Wolfingham's not such a big town."

"No, but I don't know anybody in it."

"You can meet people."

"Yes. I can meet people. Slowly. And I can hope, after two or three years of meeting people, that I meet the person we're looking for. Especially if she hasn't moved away by then, or dyed her hair a different color, or joined a nunnery in Tibet."

Bernard ran a hand through his hair until it stood up like a cockatoo's plume. "We need help."

"I would say so."

"Bentley."

"I guess."

"Do you think he has any chance at all of finding her?"

"Well, he has more than we have. He might know who she is from the description—after all, he lives there."

"A sad day, when you have to ask Bentley for help," said Bernard.

"I agree."

"Do you want to call him, or should I?"

"You do it, please. The soup is boiling over and the muffins are burning. I can smell them from out here."

Bernard was horrified. "Well, get them out of the oven, then, Snooky. You can't eat burned muffins."

As Snooky left the room, he saw Bernard reaching slowly and reluctantly for the telephone.

"Where did you say you got this information from?"

"From a concerned citizen," replied Snooky.

Bentley looked sceptical. He was settled like a toadstool, his short legs dangling off the floor, on the sofa next to the fireplace. "Who?"

"I can't say. Surely you understand that, Detective. I have to protect my sources. What kind of weaselly faced informer would I be otherwise?"

"A blond woman." Bentley jotted it down on his pad. "She was described to you as—?"

"As a brazen hussy."

"And she and Bobby Fuller were seen walking together on the main street in Wolfingham?"

"Yes."

"She might not even live there. They might have arranged to meet there because it's close by. I don't see how I can find her. This description is hardly complete. How old was she, for instance?"

"I don't know, Detective. My sources didn't say. I got the feeling she was around Bobby's age, though, or maybe a little younger."

Bentley shook his head slowly.

Bernard, from the massive armchair which he favored, said, "I would suggest that you search Bobby Fuller's apartment. There might be something with her name on it, or an address—something."

"We've already been all through his apartment. Nothing there."

"Yes, but you weren't looking for another girlfriend's address. It might have been overlooked, or tossed aside. Why don't you go through it again?"

Bentley got to his feet. "Not a bad idea. I'll do that." The door banged shut behind him.

Maya came in a few minutes later with the groceries and a worried expression on her face. "Was that Detective Bentley I passed on the way up here?"

Bernard nodded.

"Why was he here again? Hasn't he tortured us enough?"

"We called him and invited him over."

Maya leaned against the kitchen door. "What in the world possessed you to do that, darling?"

Bernard briefly outlined Snooky's conversation with

Charlotte. Snooky lay on a sofa nearby, holding Misty on his chest and gazing deep into her soft red-brown eyes. He was murmuring to her under his breath.

When Bernard was finished, Maya said, "Using some more of your famous charm on that helpless old lady, Snooks?"

"I can't help it, My. Women are fascinated by me. Look at Misty, here. I have her spellbound."

"She's not spellbound." Bernard pushed aside the red shaggy hair over Misty's face. "She's asleep."

"Well, she's asleep *now*. But five minutes ago she was spellbound."

Misty snored pleasantly.

"So Bobby had another girlfriend," said Maya.

"Yes."

"This puts a whole new wrinkle on it, doesn't it, darling?"

"Yes."

"Do you think this mystery woman could have been the one who killed him?"

Bernard gazed out the window and scratched his beard thoughtfully. "It's possible. Yes, it's possible."

"Do you think . . . well, do you think that Irma had any *idea?*"

"About this other woman, you mean? No, I'm sure she didn't."

"Why not?"

"Because she wouldn't have gotten engaged to Bobby if she knew about it. And I'm sure he went to great lengths to keep his two lives totally separate."

"Do you think Detective Bentley has any chance of finding out who she is?"

"I doubt it," Bernard said bitterly. "Given his abilities."

There was a long silence. The fire leaped and crackled, reaching tendrils of flame up the blackened chimney. Snooky sighed, the weight of Misty on his chest and her placid breathing lulling him to sleep. Bernard sat quietly, his eyelids drooping. Maya sat on the edge of his armchair, curled up in the crook of his arm, half-asleep.

After a while, Bernard picked up a small notebook and a large green Magic Marker that lay on the coffee table in front of him. He opened the notebook and uncapped the pen. Maya, on his shoulder, was fully asleep now. She sighed and murmured something. He shifted his weight so he was more comfortable, put his arm closely around her, and with his other hand wrote:

JLSY?

This stood for "jealousy." He looked at that for a long time.

Then, in rapid succession:

MNY? ("money")

GRLFRND ("girlfriend")

DD SMON ELS NO? ("did someone else know?")

and

GRD ("greed")

It always came down to greed. So many things did. It was a shame, Bernard thought. He suspected that if Bobby Fuller had been a little less careful about concealing his mystery girlfriend, he might still be alive. The killer might not have seen Bobby as a threat if they had known about his other life. On the other hand, it was possible that this girlfriend was the one who finished him off. She might have heard about the engagement and lost her head.

He made a few more notes in large green letters, and sat looking in self-satisfied absorption at his notebook while the fire burned low in the grate. Around him Snooky, Misty and Maya slumbered peacefully, their faces relaxed and quiet. Misty's mouth was open and she was dribbling happily all over Snooky's newly washed shirt. Bernard looked up from his notes and smiled.

For the next few days, life in the cabin went on as usual, except that Bernard grew increasingly fretful. He gnawed on his pencils until Maya remarked that he was making himself a candidate for lead poisoning. He switched to gnawing on his erasers. He decapitated the bunny eraser and gnawed thoughtfully on first one ear, then the other.

"What's with Bernard?" Snooky asked Maya one night in the kitchen, after dinner. "I don't get it."

"He's got murder on the brain. He's thinking more about Bobby's death than he is about his work."

"Watching him chew on the furniture is making me ill."

"He's not sleeping too well, either."

Finally Maya, in irritation, suggested that Bernard call the police station and find out what was happening. "Honestly, if it's bothering you so much, Bernard, then do something about it. I can't stand seeing you like this."

Bernard looked up, a pink bunny leg dangling from his mouth. "Like what?"

"Like this. Here, I'll dial for you." She picked up the phone book, riffled through it, then dialed rapidly. "Here. You talk."

"Is Detective Bentley there, please? . . . Hello? . . . Yes. Thank you." Bernard waited. "Detective Bentley? . . . Bernard Woodruff here. I was wondering . . . uh-huh . . . uh-huh . . . uh-huh . . . Oh. I see . . . Uh-huh, yes, I see. Thank you . . . Really? . . . Thank you very much." He hung up.

"Well?"

"Nothing," Bernard said heavily. "He said they're 'pursuing some clues,' but I could tell he has nothing. There was a sort of surly, defeated tone to his voice."

"Maybe he always sounds like that."

"Yes, but this was worse than usual."

"I'm sorry, sweetheart."

"That's all right. It's none of my business, anyway." He turned away and bit off one of the rabbit paws savagely. "I've got my work to do. I don't have time for this."

Sarah and Snooky were in bed together the next afternoon, in her room upstairs at the Ditmar mansion. This was a small, functional closetlike space, filled with stuffed toys from her childhood, small framed watercolors, and study guides for the law boards, which she was planning to take soon. Irma had gone off into town to do some shopping. Gertie, as always, was out in the woods.

"So Irma's up and about," Snooky said. He ran one finger down Sarah's delicate profile. Her red hair was spread out over the pillow, catching the afternoon light in glints of flame. She was gazing contentedly up at the ceiling. Sarah, he had discovered, was freckled all over, her skin a pale apricot, her body sinewy and strong.

"Yes. I think that visit from the Grunwalds helped to revive her. Got her back in fighting trim, she said. Her heart's much better, and she seems to have more energy."

"Good."

"Irma's very strong mentally. I know she doesn't seem that way, but she is. All she needs is a challenge to get her going."

"Uh-huh." Snooky was not interested in Irma's mental strength. He played thoughtfully with Sarah's hair.

"How are things out at the cabin?"

Snooky shrugged. "Bernard's even more irritable than usual, if possible. He can't seem to get Bobby's death out of his mind."

"Really?" She crossed her arms behind her head. "That's funny. To me it seems like it never happened. I mean, like that whole episode with Bobby and Aunt Irma never happened. Life is just going on as usual."

"Uh-huh. Sarah, I was wondering . . . you never heard anything about—well, about any other woman that Bobby was involved with, did you?"

Sarah looked startled. "Another woman? No, nothing. Have you . . . what have you heard?"

"Just wondering. You don't think that anyone else in your family knew about anything like that, do you?"

"No," she said positively. "I'm sure they didn't. News

like that would get around. Nobody here can keep a secret. Are you sure about this, Snooky?"

"No, no. It's just an idea . . . an idea that Bernard and I had. He wondered if Bobby could have been interested in somebody else."

"I don't think so. He always seemed very devoted to Aunt Irma."

"Uh-huh. Listen, something else has been on my mind. How would you like to come out to the cabin and stay with me for a couple of days? Irma doesn't need you as much now, and we never get any time together alone."

"What about Maya and Bernard?"

"They wouldn't mind. They're my guests, anyway. It's *my* cabin, remember?"

"You're sure?"

"Of course I'm sure. Don't be ridiculous. They'd be delighted. You're one of the first girlfriends I've ever had that they both liked."

"Well, in that case, I accept. I'd love to get out of the house for a while, if you're certain I'd be welcome."

"Don't be ridiculous," said Snooky, leaning back on the pillow and gathering her into his arms.

That evening, he cornered Maya over the dishes and said worriedly, "My?"

"Mmmhmmm?"

"Do you think it'd be okay if Sarah came out here to stay with me for a couple of days?"

Maya gave him an amused glance. "Of course it would. Why are you asking me?"

"You're sure you wouldn't mind?"

"Don't be stupid, Snooky. What you do is your own business. You're an adult, aren't you?"

"I know that. I know that, My. I'm just asking."

"Well, it's fine with me. I like Sarah. She's different from your other girlfriends. She seems normal. Ask Bernard about it if you have some kind of problem. I guarantee you he won't care one way or the other. As long as his meals get served on time, Bernard can ignore pretty much everything else."

"Okay."

The conversation with Bernard was short and to the point.

"Bernard?"

"Yes?"

"I'd like to ask you a question."

Bernard leaned back from his typing table and regarded his brother-in-law wearily. "Yes?"

"Would it bother you if Sarah came to stay with us for a while?"

Bernard raised his eyebrows. "Here?"

"Yes."

"In the cabin?"

"Yes."

"With you?"

"Yes."

"No."

"No, it wouldn't bother you?"

"No."

"Are you sure?"

"Yes. Why would it bother me?" Bernard said irritably. "You're bothering me much more right now by interrupting my work, for instance. Is this conversation over?"

"It is on my side."

"Then good-bye, Snooky."

"Good-bye."

"Has Bernard ever considered becoming a therapist?" Snooky asked his sister later that evening. "He's so empathetic, you know. I just wondered."

Maya was correcting a copy of her latest article. She had her reading glasses on and was huddled next to a lamp. "Bernard is empathetic, in his own way. Did he mind about Sarah?"

"No."

1 0 5

"I told you."

"I know you did."

"When will she be coming?"

"Tomorrow night, I think."

"Good."

"Does Bernard listen to you when you talk?" Snooky asked plaintively. "Just wondering."

"Uh-huh."

"I don't understand it. I don't get it, My. How could he be such different things to different people?"

Maya, absorbed in her article, did not reply. Snooky sighed and picked up the dog.

"It's just you and me, Misty. Nobody else around here pays any attention to us. They don't care what we do."

Misty, hanging in midair, regarded him placidly.

"Misty has very beautiful eyes. Have you ever noticed that, My?"

Maya nodded absently.

"Her eyes remind me of Bernard's. Sort of a deep, soulful brown."

Maya thoughtfully corrected a mistake with a large red pencil.

"I'm going to go out back and shoot myself," Snooky said, unwinding from his chair. "So long, Maya."

Maya brushed back a wisp of hair from her face. "So long, Snooky," she said kindly. Snooky sighed again and went into the kitchen to work on a lemon meringue pie he was preparing for the next day.

The next evening, after Sarah had arrived, they all gathered around the fireplace after dinner. There was a storm blowing up outside, and the wind whipped around the cabin, howling in through the cracks. Snooky, sprawled on the floor, stared in fascination at the leaping flames. Sometimes, if he looked hard enough, he could see fire lizards, eagles whose wings were ablaze, armies of tiny men moving jerkily through flaming fields. Around him everyone was quiet, lulled by the enormous meal and the heat. Sometimes, Snooky felt, if he tried hard enough, he could see the past or even the future. Sarah, lying next to him, leaned her head against his shoulder. Her hair was the same color as the flames. He put an arm around her and held her close.

"This is how life should be lived," he said. "Roughing it in the wild, close to nature, close to our roots."

"This is life on the edge, all right," remarked Maya.

"I don't understand why I've never moved out into the wilderness before. I feel as though I've found myself."

"You're difficult to locate," Maya said dryly. "Sometimes your true self is out in the wilds, sometimes it's living in the big city. It changes so often."

"That's not true, Maya."

"It is true. You're a wanderer, Snooks—a free spirit."

Bernard, from his seat on the couch, snorted derisively.

Snooky gave himself up to contemplation of the flame shapes that were forming in the depths of the fire. The little marching men were clearer now, banners waving, legs moving rapidly as the flames fled upward into the blackened chimney. The fire eagle spread its wings and soared upward, vanishing with a pop. Faces appeared and disappeared, loved faces from his past, swimming before him in a reddened haze of memory. His head drooped gradually. He was nearly asleep when he heard Maya say, her voice rich with amusement,

"There he goes. He used to hypnotize himself every winter night in front of the fire when we were growing up. It would scare William to death. He'd go into a kind of trance, and have trouble waking up. I think he's psychic. I bet he could channel spirits if he wanted to."

Bernard glanced around at the darkened cabin. Their shadows were leaping monstrously on the far walls. "Don't mention spirits, Maya. Not here. Not at night."

"Oh, *Bernard.*"

"I mean it."

"Bernard lived in a haunted house when he was little," Maya explained to Sarah. "The spirit of his great-aunt went wailing up and down the stairs. And there was another one in the kitchen who used to rattle the pots and pans. Isn't that right, sweetheart?"

Bernard said sourly, "Yes."

"Tell Sarah about it. It's fascinating."

"No. It's nothing."

"Oh, please tell," said Sarah, sitting up and linking her arms around her knees. "Please."

"No."

"It was his great-aunt Sadie," Maya said. "She left her house to Bernard's father, who was her favorite nephew. Isn't that right, sweetheart? Bernard lived in it while he was growing up. It was a big old rambling place, with the wind blowing in through the cracks, and on winter nights like tonight his father used to tell his mother that he could hear his aunt Sadie roaming up and down the stairs. Bernard's parents would laugh about it, but poor Bernard would be frightened to death. He was only a little boy at the time. Sometimes his father would say that he could hear Sadie's mother—that was his grandmother—in the kitchen, cooking up a storm, the way she used to when she was alive. Poor Bernard would lie in bed night after night, listening to the stairs creak and thinking he heard the pots and pans rattling in the kitchen."

"I hated that house," said Bernard grimly. "When I was ten, my parents sold it and moved to a modern development. It was the happiest day of my life. I never had any trouble sleeping after that. For all I know, Aunt Sadie and her mother are still in the old house, cooking and walking the stairs."

"That's a poignant story, Bernard," said Snooky, sitting up.

Maya gave him an amused look. "So you're awake now, Snooks? Any psychic dreams this time? Can you read our fortunes?"

"Nothing psychic this time, My. Just images. Fire lizards, eagles, things like that." He fell silent, brooding.

"William used to hate when you did that."

"William hated when I did anything."

"William is afraid of anything he doesn't understand," said Maya. "The supernatural. Trances. Ghosts. Snooky."

"William has a very limited imagination. The only thing he truly understands is money. How to handle it, what to do with it, how to make lots of it."

"You never learned that last bit," said Maya.

"No. I never did."

The wind roared outside, and the windows rattled. Bernard glanced about uneasily. "I'm going to bed, Maya. Wake me when the storm is over."

"Good night, darling."

"Good night."

Much later, in the small hours of the night, Bernard awoke with a creeping feeling of fear. He lay unmoving, straining his ears to listen, his eyes open and staring in the darkness, his nerves on fire. There was something that had awakened him . . . a bumping noise of some kind . . . *somewhere in the cabin!*

Visions of his great-aunt Sadie as he had imagined her in his childhood, her image drawn from a small black-and-white Victorian photograph that his father had kept lovingly enshrined in the family album, floated in front of his mind's eye. Her stubborn jaw, pug nose, protuberant eyes and graying hair, which was parted in the middle and swept unforgivingly backwards to an unseen locus on the back of her head—all the features that used to haunt his nights when he was small—came back to him vividly. The fact that her eye was kindly and her face, however ugly, had a gentle look to it, had not made an impression on his boyhood mind at all. To him she was the monster of his dreams, sweeping up and down the stairs, bumping into the furniture, wailing his name through the night: *"Bernard . . . Bernard, come to me . . . Bernard!"* And her nightmare mother, cooking up a storm in the kitchen—to Bernard's childhood mind, this inadvertent phrase of his father's meant that his great-grandmother was cooking up a real storm, busily mixing up thunderclouds, stirring the cauldron with lightning bolts, boiling up rain. He always saw her with her white head surrounded by black rumbling clouds and mist, cackling wildly as she mixed up a hell's brew of a storm, stirring the broth with broken tree trunks, adding a touch of fog and mist, seasoning it all with thunderclaps. To this day, a fierce thunderstorm evoked images in his mind of his great-grandmother bent over a black kettle that raged and boiled as the lightning bolts crackled their eerie path to the ground.

He lay still, breathing loudly and nervously. All at once there was a tremendous *thump* against the wall of his bedroom. The walls shuddered and creaked. Bernard gasped. From somewhere in the cabin came a faint groan. Bernard broke out in a cold sweat. He put out a trembling hand and touched Maya's shoulder, partly to make sure she was still alive, partly to awaken her.

"Maya?" he breathed.

She rolled over in her sleep. "Mmmmpththmph?"

"Maya, wake up. *Wake up.*"

"Mmmhththktph?"

"Wake up!"

She opened a drowsy eye. "Whatsit? Whatsmatter?"

"Maya . . . *do you hear that?*"

Suddenly the *thump* came again, louder than before. There was a faint, strangled cry from somewhere else in the cabin. The walls shuddered, then were still.

"Maya," Bernard said, barely breathing, "Maya . . . *what is that?*"

To his astonishment, his wife began to laugh quietly. She rolled over and drew the coverlet up to her chin. "Bernard, sometimes you amaze me," she whispered.

"What?"

"Darling," she said drowsily, "please go back to sleep. It's nothing. It'll stop soon."

"How do you know?"

"Because I'm psychic, like my brother. I guarantee it'll stop. Now go back to sleep, sweetheart. It's—" she sleepily checked the alarm clock, which glowed faintly in the darkness, "it's four o'clock in the morning. Snooky will have us up at eight for breakfast. Go to sleep."

"*Maya,*" whispered Bernard in agony, but she had already dozed off. He lay still, his body lathered in sweat, his ears straining for the slightest sound. There was another crash, and an eerie cry. He shuddered down to his bones. What if it wasn't the ghost of Aunt Sadie . . . what if it was an intruder, slitting Snooky and Sarah's throats, all as mere practice before he came after Maya and himself? How could Maya be so calm?

There was a muffled *thump* against the wall, followed by a stifled groan. Bernard lay still for a moment, then threw off the covers and padded nervously over to the wall, mincing across the room on cold feet. The wall shook as two bodies hurtled into it from the other side. There was the sound of muffled laughter, a few giggles and whispers, and then everything was still.

Bernard felt very, very grim. He padded back to bed, examined the clockface, its phosphorescent hands telling him it was 4:10 A.M., and switched on the reading lamp.

"Maya," he said.

"Yes?"

"It's four-ten in the morning."

She rolled over and smiled at him sleepily. "I can't help that, Bernard. They're young and energetic. We were like that once, too. Remember? Now turn off the light, darling, and try to get some sleep. You're going to be cranky all day tomorrow otherwise."

"I'm going to be cranky, all right. I have something to be cranky about."

There was a crash, and more muffled laughter from the other bedroom.

"Maya."

"Yes, darling?"

"I want to go home. *Now.*"

There was more laughter, and now they could hear Sarah's voice clearly, raised in a kind of gasp. "Oh, Snooky . . . honestly . . . I don't think that's possible—!" It

111

ended in a gasp of laughter, and the muffled sound of his voice.

"I don't think we can go home now, Bernard. It's so early in the morning. I wouldn't trust you to drive in the state you're in."

"What are they doing in there, Maya? Inhaling laughing gas?"

"Please go back to sleep."

"I think they're doing something illegal." Bernard switched off the light and hunched down underneath the covers. Misty, in bed between the two of them, snored pleasantly, her sleep undisturbed by Snooky's nocturnal activities. "I'm going to have a little talk with Snooky in the morning."

"They're young and in love, Bernard. Leave them alone. We've stayed up all night, too."

"Not where someone could *hear* us."

"I'm sure they don't know. Good night, darling."

"Good night."

Bernard stayed up, plotting his revenge, until he finally dozed off around five.

Bernard, inventive as he was, and with all the time in the world to think about it, solved the problem neatly by the following evening. He got into bed, kissed his wife a loving good-night, turned out the lights and waited. Maya drifted off immediately, her hands tucked underneath the pillow, on her face the gentle, dreamy expression that Bernard loved. A shaft of moonlight slanted in through the curtains and picked out her features, making her look very pale and ethereal, the sharp bones in her cheeks heightened by shadows, her face as narrow and mysterious in sleep as an elf's. Bernard waited. At last his patience was rewarded. There was a crash against the wall, and quiet snorts of laughter. Bernard threw off the covers, sat up in bed, and said at the top of his lungs,

"WHAT'S THAT, MAYA? WHAT'S THAT? DO YOU HEAR SOMETHING?"

Maya turned and murmured something in her sleep. "Leave m'lone. What? Hmmtphph?"

"MAYA, WAKE UP. I THINK YOUR BROTHER IS BE-ING KILLED. THERE'S A TERRIBLE NOISE FROM HIS ROOM."

This had the desired effect. There was a sudden, total silence from the other side of the wall. Bernard imagined Snooky and his girlfriend startled from their absorption in each other, lying in bed with their heads up, eyes startled, ears straining to hear.

"MAYA, I THINK I SHOULD GO INVESTIGATE. THERE WAS A TERRIBLE NOISE. IT SOUNDED LIKE SOMEBODY WAS BEING KILLED, OR LIKE A PIG BEING STUCK. DON'T STOP ME. I'M GOING TO GO OVER THERE. SOMEBODY SHOULD WARN SNOOKY."

Maya pulled the covers up over her head.

Bernard listened. There was a deep, tranquil silence from the other side of the wall; the proverbial silence of the graveyard. He smiled grimly.

"ALL RIGHT, IF YOU THINK I SHOULDN'T, I WON'T, BUT I'M TELLING YOU, THERE WAS SOME-THING. SOME KIND OF STRANGE NOISE. ALL RIGHT. GOOD NIGHT, MAYA."

Maya giggled sleepily.

"SLEEP WELL. ARE YOU SURE IT WASN'T ANY-THING? ALL RIGHT. GOOD NIGHT."

Bernard lay down and plumped the pillow up around his head. There was silence from the direction of Snooky's bedroom. Outside his window, a lone owl hooted eerily. There was the sound of the wind in the trees, the owl, his own and Maya's breathing, Misty's snoring, and nothing else. Over the cabin, peace and quiet reigned.

6

Sarah stayed at the cabin for a few days—during which time Bernard's sleep was undisturbed—and then thanked them all and left. "I really have to get back," she explained to Snooky. "Irma still needs me, and God knows what Gertie's been up to. I know they can't fend for themselves in that big house."

"They did fine while you were in college."

"I know, but it's different now. Irma still isn't herself."

"All right. I'll drive you back. Are you sure you're not letting Bernard drive you away?"

"Not at all," said Sarah. "Bernard is . . . is a poppet."

"Sarah says you're a poppet," Snooky said later that day. Bernard looked offended.

"She says she enjoys your company."

Bernard shrugged.

"Yes," said Snooky. "I don't get it either. What are your plans for today?"

"We're going antiquing," said Maya.

"Antiquing? What an excellent idea."

"Want to come along? You might find something interesting."

"Not me. I don't have any place to put anything. You know me, Maya."

Maya nodded. With his succession of rented or borrowed homes, Snooky had learned the difficult lesson of keeping his possessions to a minimum, like a Zen monk. He typically appeared on her front doorstep with a brown paper bag containing his toothbrush, a few items of clothing, and little more. He supplemented any deficiencies in his wardrobe by borrowing freely from Bernard's.

"There are some good stores around here. The two of you should go take a look. You can't come to Vermont and not go shopping for antiques, anyway. It's against the law."

"Give me the names of some stores we can go to, will you?"

Snooky tilted back his chair. "Let's see. There's the Pink Boar in Lyle. You can't miss it. It's very distinctive. It's got this enormous scarlet pig painted on a sign above the door. You go past the main square and turn right on Oak Street. And in Wolfingham, there's a whole street full of shops. Ask anyone there, they'll be able to direct you."

"All right, Snooks. We'll be back in time for dinner."

"Somehow," said Snooky, "I had guessed that."

"What's this, Maya?"

Bernard held up a small polished spindle of wood. It had a rounded knob on either end and fit snugly into the palm of his hand.

"I don't know, darling."

"There are two of them. Like miniature dumbbells."

"I've never seen anything like them before."

"Or how about this?" It was a tiny, but unexpectedly heavy, black metal box with the name SYLVIA in raised metal letters on the top.

"I have no idea. I can't imagine what Sylvia used it for."

Bernard pawed through the pile of clutter in the back of the shop. "This is great, Maya. Look at this." He showed her a small white ashtray with a red crown in the middle. Underneath the crown were the gold letters E II R. Around the letters was a golden scroll that read, THE QUEEN'S SILVER JUBILEE, 1952–1977.

Bernard was delighted. "It's English, of course. The Queen's Jubilee. This is terrific stuff, Maya."

"Add it to the pile, darling."

They were in the Pink Boar in Lyle. For the past half hour they had been shuffling around the limited floor space, edging their way past long cherrywood tables and piles of rickety wooden chairs. There were chests of drawers, tables, chairs, desks, broken lamps and crockery. In the back, Bernard had discovered, to his joy, a huge cardboard box filled with odds and ends. Now he was snuffling through it, unearthing strange and unlikely objects with small whimpers of delight.

"Look at this, Maya. What is this?"

Maya regarded the latest object wearily. It was a long brass utensil with a rounded spoon at one end and a fork at the other. "I don't have the faintest idea."

"It's great, isn't it?" Bernard spun it experimentally. It was nearly two feet long from fork to spoon. "I could hang it on the wall of my study."

The walls of Bernard's study, and in fact the study itself, were so cluttered that Maya doubted he would be able to find room for this latest acquisition. "Fine. I'll be over here, by those chairs. I could use some extra chairs."

She left Bernard with his hands buried in the cardboard box, his eyes aglow, and moved over to the pile of chairs. Bernard gravitated naturally to the small and unusual objects, while her forte was the large furniture. She was disentangling one of the chairs from the pile for a closer look, when there was a strangled cry of joy from the back of the store.

"Maya? Maya, come look at this."

When she reached her husband, he was sitting on the floor, oblivious to the layers of dust and clutter all around him. In his lap, he was gently cradling an antique typewriter. He held it up for her to see. It was one of the very old manual ones, with a dull black exterior and tiny raised round keys. There was a roll of ancient typewriter ribbon hanging disconsolately off the spool. It looked as if it had not seen the light of day for perhaps thirty years.

"It's very nice, sweetheart. You've been looking for one of those, haven't you?"

Bernard cradled it on his lap and stroked the keys lovingly. "This is it, Maya. Exactly what I wanted. I'll put it on the bookcase in my room. Once I shine it up, it'll be beautiful. Or maybe it's more interesting if I leave it this way. It's one of the old ones, Maya. One of the early ones. Isn't it something?"

She admitted cheerfully that it was indeed something.

Half an hour later they paid for their purchases and left. The stores in Wolfingham proved to be a disappointment, and they were back at the cabin by late afternoon. Bernard arranged his newly acquired possessions in a semicircle on the floor. Then he stood in front of them and gloated openly.

"I've never seen anything like it," said Snooky. "Look at him. It's pathetic."

Bernard picked up one of the wooden spindles and began to play with it, tossing it from hand to hand.

"And it's all nothing but trash," said Snooky in amazement. "Except for that typewriter, maybe. But everything else is just trash. Look at this." He picked up the Queen's Silver Jubilee ashtray. "I can't believe my eyes."

Bernard took it away from him. He put it lovingly back on the floor and continued to gloat silently.

"Does he always get this kind of junk?" Snooky asked.

"Yes." Maya was standing by the window, drinking coffee, gazing out into the deepening twilight.

"Did you get anything for yourself, My?"

"I found a chair. It's in the back of the car. We can bring it in later. It probably shouldn't be left out in the cold."

Bernard picked up the ashtray, put it down, then picked up the metal box named SYLVIA. He picked up the brass fork-

and-spoon combination, held it aloft triumphantly like a trident and spun it once or twice over his head. He smiled fiercely.

"He's like a little boy," Snooky remarked. "A child at Christmas."

Bernard picked up the pair of wooden spindles and hefted them over his head, up and down, up and down. Maya took another sip of coffee.

"I have some news that will interest you," she said. "Detective Bentley is here."

Not even this disturbed Bernard's concentration. He was twirling the spindles thoughtfully, one in each hand, testing their weight.

"He's parked his car out front, and he's getting out of it now."

"Lock the door and turn out all the lights, Maya," said Snooky cheerfully. "We can all hide under the table until he's given up and gone away." However, he did not budge from his position, supine on the sofa.

"He's here." Maya put her cup down and went to the front door. "How nice to see you, Detective."

Bentley grunted and shoved past her. "Have some questions for the two of you," he said to Bernard and Snooky. Bernard, lost in contemplation of his new treasures, did not look at him.

"Please sit down, Detective," said Snooky. "Make yourself at home. What can we do for you today?"

"I need more information about this alleged girlfriend of Bobby Fuller's."

"I don't have any more information. I've already told you everything."

Bentley looked unhappy. "I can't find her based on a physical description of her as a 'brazen hussy.' It's not enough."

"I can't help that, Detective. That's how she was described to me. You didn't find anything useful in Bobby's apartment?"

118

"No. Nothing—no names, no addresses, nothing. He was careful, all right. If this woman you're talking about really exists, that is."

"I only know what I've told you so far."

"It's not enough."

"I'm more sorry than I can possibly say. There's nothing I can do about that."

"You can give me the name of the person who saw her. Your source may know more about it than you do. That wouldn't be hard."

Snooky gazed at him reproachfully. "I can't do that. You can pull out my tongue and flay me alive, but I can't do that. It's not right."

"I wouldn't say who had told me," Bentley said cunningly.

"No."

Bentley sighed. "There's nothing else you can tell me?"

"She was blond, around Bobby's age, maybe younger, and attractive enough to be described as a hussy. They were seen together on the main street in Wolfingham. That's it."

"It's not very much," Bentley said heavily. His shoulders drooped. Snooky, looking at him, realized that the little detective was honestly depressed over how the investigation was going. He was overcome by a sudden friendly wave of compassion.

"Listen," he said. "I can't give you the name of my source, but I can try to get more information. If I come up with anything, I'll give you a call. How's that?"

Bentley nodded. "Thank you."

"You're very welcome."

The next afternoon, Snooky stationed himself by the massive pile of Maine potatoes at Harry's Market. He waited patiently. He knew that Charlotte Grunwald came in most days around three o'clock to do her shopping. He had run into her several times since their conversation; she had seemed nervous and apprehensive and not at all talkative since then, although she had flashed him a shy smile before she hurried away.

Promptly at midafternoon, Charlotte appeared like a gray smoky vision at the door of Harry's Market and Fresh Produce Stand. She was wearing, as always, her gray cap and gray wool winter coat, firmly buttoned up to her pointy chin. She carried a basket in one arm and her purse slung over her shoulder. This time, however, she was accompanied by an elderly white-haired man with deep blue eyes. Snooky smiled affably and made his way over to the heaping bins of apples near the door.

"Charlotte. How nice to see you."

"Oh, Snooky." She seemed flustered. "Hello. You know Frank Vanderwoort, our neighbor, don't you?"

Snooky gave him a friendly nod. "Hello, Frank."

"Hello, Snooky."

"Charlotte, there's something I wanted to ask you about, if you don't mind . . ."

"I'll leave you two to chat," said the white-haired man, and moved away toward the vegetable display.

Charlotte regarded him nervously out of the corner of her eye. "What is it?"

"It's about that woman you described to me the other day—"

She gave a small half-gasp. "Oh, Snooky, I felt so *terrible* afterward. I really shouldn't have done that. I don't know what came over me. It was *none* of my business . . ."

"Oh, I understand completely, Charlotte. If you're uncomfortable and you don't want to talk about it anymore, that's fine with me."

"Well . . . I don't think I really *should* . . ."

"I'm sorry for bringing it up. Can I help you with the vegetables?"

Charlotte stood on one foot, storklike, and stared at him, her mind clicking over slowly. Her curiosity was piqued. "Well . . . what is it you wanted to know? I really shouldn't talk about it, but since you bring it up . . ."

"Oh, it's nothing. Just idle curiosity."

Charlotte peered at him, waiting.

"To be honest with you, I've been wondering what Bobby's girlfriend really looked like. I mean, 'brazen hussy' isn't much of a description, is it?"

"It's a perfectly good description. That's what she was."

"How could you tell?"

She dismissed him with a contemptuous glance. *Men,* her look said clearly. *Men! How could I tell? They simply don't understand!*

"I know I'm being stupid," Snooky said. "If you could just describe her a little more fully . . ."

"Well, she was wearing an orange-colored dress, much too loud and truly tasteless, if you want my opinion. Very lowcut in front. She had an open cardigan on, but that didn't really—well, it didn't really cover anything up, if you know what I mean." Charlotte sniffed disapprovingly. "A hussy. And she had short blond hair, curled all over. She was a little overweight. Plump, I mean. And she was short, around Bobby's height."

"How old was she?"

"Oh, I don't know. Around his age, I would think. Late thirties. Lots of dark eyeshadow and mascara and bright red lips. No—no *restraint* at all." Poor Charlotte, who had been forced by circumstances that she had never chosen—the personalities of her father and older sister—to be restrained her whole life, shuddered in distaste. "No restraint, no taste, simply—simply *flamboyance.* She had a round face and I'm sure her hair was dyed. Why, now, it's funny how it all comes back to me when I think about it. Yes, her hair was dyed—it was too yellow, you know, no highlights in it, all the same shade." Charlotte sniffed again and unconsciously lifted a hand to pat her own dull, graying mop of hair. "She had her arm through Bobby's, and they were laughing and talking. I never saw him laughing like that with Irma," she added meanly, then blushed at her own words.

"You're amazing, do you know that, Charlotte? I think

you have a photographic memory. I really do. All those details, just like that."

She preened and began to glow, heating up from within like an incandescent sun. "Oh. Do you think so? That's very kind. You know, it surprises me too, how it all comes back so clearly. It's as though I can almost see her now."

"It's a gift, Charlotte. A gift. You should be very proud."

"Oh . . . *oh!*" She stood gazing at him with the sheepish smile of a young girl. He thanked her and hurried away, leaving her pink-faced and pleased, standing in the aisle of Harry's Market all by herself, glowing with deep inward warmth on a cold winter's day.

"You are a heartless flatterer," Maya said disapprovingly.

"I know."

"You should be taken out back and your head should be boiled in oil."

"No doubt." Snooky ran his finger down a list. "Dyed blond hair, short curls. Overweight. Lots of makeup. Short, around Bobby's height. Loud, low-cut orange dress. Big breasts."

"How do you know she had big breasts? Charlotte couldn't have brought herself to say that?"

"In so many words, Maya. In so many words."

Maya was peeling potatoes over the sink. "Bobby didn't seem attractive enough to me to have two women falling all over him."

"Women are a strange species, Maya. There's no accounting for their tastes. Bernard, for instance, found somebody to marry him."

"Bernard is a very handsome, a very sexy man."

Snooky gazed at her reproachfully. "Please, Maya. Please. You cannot imagine in your wildest dreams how profoundly I don't want to hear you talk about him that way. Do you think this will be enough for Bentley to find her?"

"The mystery woman?"

"Yes."

"I doubt it, Snooks. He hasn't been able to find her so far. He doesn't seem to be able to follow up on things very well."

Snooky gazed at his list despondently. "Well, I don't think I have any choice. I'll have to give him a call and read this to him. Maybe it'll help, who knows."

"When you're done, come back and help me with the potatoes."

Detective Bentley was, as Snooky had hoped he would be, profoundly grateful for the information.

"That's it?" he barked.

"Yes, that's it."

"That's all you got?"

"I think it's quite a lot, myself," snapped Snooky, his hackles rising.

"Okay." Bentley slammed down the phone. Snooky came back into the kitchen with a thunderous look on his face.

"There is no gratitude in this world," he informed Maya. He took the peeler away from her and picked up a potato from the basket near the sink. "No gratitude, Maya, do you hear me?"

"I hear you, Snooks."

"Why did I volunteer to help Detective Bentley? Was I not in my right mind?"

"I would imagine it was a moment's feverish hallucination."

"Yes, that must have been it," said Snooky, beginning to scrape with short, angry strokes. "That must have been it."

Snooky spent the next few days over at Hugo's Folly, helping Sarah with the meals. Irma was up and about, and the three of them spent a lot of time together, chatting in the kitchen, having tea in the living room. Gertie popped in for meals, but otherwise was, like the wildlife she pursued, rarely to be glimpsed. She would come into the kitchen, unload various objects from her pockets—usually a messy-looking collection of twigs, bits of moss, brown leaves and feathers—and stand rubbing her hands together over them.

"Naked miterwort," she once announced brusquely to Snooky as he passed by her on his way into the dining room.

"Pardon me?"

"Naked miterwort. I'm sure of it. It's an herb, you know. A perennial. Your sister would have heard of it. Of course this bit is all blasted, but then it is winter." She brooded over the tiny twig in her hand.

"How fascinating," Snooky said kindly.

"Yes. I've been coming up with the most amazing specimens. This year is the best ever. I can't wait for spring. Miterwort flowers in April."

"What's this here?" Snooky asked, pointing at a piece of measled gray fur.

"Not sure. I think it might be rat."

"Rat?"

"There are rats in these woods, didn't you know that? Norway rats. This is my greatest find so far." She held up a long feather reverently. "Do you know what this is?"

"A feather?"

"Don't be stupid. It's from a goshawk. An honest-to-God goshawk. One of the biggest birds I've ever seen in these parts. May have come down from Canada. Don't know what it's doing here. It was a young one, too. Gorgeous." She twirled the feather, a dreamy expression in her eyes.

Snooky picked over the small pile of pine cones, leaves, feathers and fur. "What's this?"

"That?" She looked at him, amused. "That's a maple leaf. You mean to say you don't recognize a maple leaf?"

"Oh."

"Pathetic, the level of botanical education they give to the young these days. I suppose you spent your college days partying and fooling around with women?"

This was, in fact, an uncannily accurate description of

the time Snooky had spent in college, but he felt obliged to defend himself. "I was interested in philosophy," he said hotly. "I read Kierkegaard."

Gertie gave him a withering glance. "Philosophy!" she said. "Philosophy is not life. Botany is life. Philosophy is— is just *words*."

With a loud harrummphing sound, she turned back to her little pile of treasured odds and ends, dismissing him.

Over lunch, Snooky remarked on how well Irma was looking. "You seem to have come back to yourself, Irma. You must be feeling better."

"I am, dear." Irma was wearing a white cashmere dress and a red scarf which matched her lipstick. Her face glowed with color, not all of it artificial, and her eyes were a bright, bright green. Her gray hair was neatly curled around her little head, every strand firmly anchored in place with hairspray.

"You do look awfully well, Aunt Irma," said Sarah, on the other side of the table.

Gertie, hunched in her chair, feeding rapaciously, not unlike one of the goshawks she was so fond of, made a kindly booming sound in agreement. Irma trilled to herself and looked pleased.

"Life goes on, my dears. Life goes on. Of course I will never really get over the terrible shock of it, but life goes on. I went on alone after Hugo's death, too."

Sarah murmured in sympathy. Gertie paused, her fork in mid-air.

"Hugo was a good man," she said.

"Oh, yes, dear . . . yes, he was. The very best."

"He was a good brother."

"So he was."

"Not right to have somebody take his place."

Irma stared at her, her eyes wide. There was a sudden palpable tension in the air, like frost, or a storm cloud moving in.

"Gertie, I've been alone now for nearly fifteen years

since Hugo passed on. You don't begrudge me my little bit of happiness, do you?"

Gertie looked embarrassed. She made a brusque waving motion with her fork and knife. "No. Sorry. Didn't mean it."

The atmosphere relaxed. Irma picked up her wineglass and began chatting about her plans for the day. "First I'll go to Harry's Market and see if he has anything good . . . then I'll go to Tiny Sam's for a cup of coffee." Tiny Sam's was a little diner in town—in fact the only diner in town. It was run by Tiny Sam himself, who always made a point of waiting on Irma when she was there. Tiny Sam was a giant of a man, nearly six and a half feet tall, weighing over three hundred pounds. "He's such a pet," she said now. "Always so kind. He sent me flowers when Bobby died, did you know that? Such a *kind* man. It's too bad he's already married."

"Aunt Irma!"

"Oh, well, dear, there's no harm in it. We all enjoy our little flirtations. And I'm very fond of Tiny Sam's wife, too."

Tiny Sam's wife was a resigned-looking little mouse of a woman who, after twenty-five years residence in Lyle, had not yet acquired a name of her own. She was known far and wide simply as "Tiny Sam's wife." She was a worn-looking woman with a pointed little face and fluffy brown hair that she had styled every week, with various unsuccessful results, at Dinah's House of Beauty, the only hairdresser's in town. The lunch counter was her domain and she ruled over it with an iron hand, scuttling back and forth between the counter and the kitchen like a rat in a very simple maze. It was known that Tiny Sam was slavishly devoted to his wife and was, despite his size, completely cowed by her. She would flick a spatula against his massive side and announce to the restaurant at large, "Got to take off this weight. Got to take off this weight, Tiny Sam." However, despite this well-meaning mantra repeated several times a day for twenty-five years, Tiny Sam never did take off any weight. Instead, he increased, slowly but with inexorable force, putting on an extra inch here, another roll of avoirdupois there. It seemed impossible that Tiny Sam's wife could even get her arms all the way around his incredible girth. Still, they seemed perfectly happy in their own way. "Got to take off this weight," she would announce joyfully every day in her rasping voice, as if the idea had just struck her. "Got to take off this weight, Tiny Sam."

"Yes, dear heart."

Irma was still detailing her plans for the day. "And after Tiny Sam's, I'll go on to the bakery and see if I can pick up a nice fresh bread for dinner. That would be lovely, wouldn't it, Sarah? Maybe a nice hot wheat loaf. And some buns for tea, and one of their cheesecakes for dessert. How does that sound?"

"Wonderful, Aunt Irma."

"I'll be in the woods," said Gertie shortly, pushing back her chair.

"I have to go myself," said Snooky. "Bernard's getting peevish because I haven't been around to cook meals for him. I promised him and Maya dinner tonight."

Sarah walked him to the door and gave him a kiss. "You'll be okay?" he asked her.

"Uh-huh. I have to study, anyway. The LSATs are coming up in a couple of months. I want to be ready."

"I'll call you tonight."

"Okay."

"How happy William would be to know that I'm going out with a lawyer, one of his own kind," said Snooky. "That's why I haven't told him about you. I know what he'd say."

"And what's that?"

"He'd ask me, 'What does she see in you?' "

"I'd like to meet William sometime. He can't be as bad as you say."

"Oh, he is. And his wife is worse."

"And his children?"

"Two little monsters, unredeemed by any of the common traits of humanity."

"Go," said Sarah, giving him a gentle push out the door. "Bernard is waiting for his dinner."

Snooky was driving down the long winding road leading from Hugo's Folly, humming contentedly to himself (the radio in his rented car was broken and he hadn't bothered to get it fixed yet), when an extraordinary sight met his eyes. There was a woman teetering down the road toward him. She was wearing three-inch spike heels and seemed barely able to keep her balance, yet she was marching along determinedly, holding onto a large blue purse slung over her shoulder. Her hair was a mass of bright blond curls, and her face was a symphony of blue eyeshadow, pink rouge and red lipstick. As she lurched along on her stiletto heels, her coat fell open to reveal a bright yellow dress and a large expanse of heaving bosom. Snooky passed her, went twenty yards farther down the road, then braked to a screeching halt. "Oh, Jesus," he muttered, and swung the car around.

When he reached her again, she was lurching along, making fairly good time on the way up to the Folly. There was a fiercely determined expression on her painted, overweight face.

Snooky rolled down the window and leaned out, slowing down to match her speed. "Hello, there," he said pleasantly.

"Get lost, creep!" she snarled.

"I wonder if I could be so bold as to offer you a lift?"

"Get lost, or I'll call the police."

"Going to Hugo's Folly?"

"None of your fuckin' business."

"I surmise that you are," Snooky said grandly, "since it's the only house on this road. Sure I can't offer you a lift?"

"Get lost, creep!"

"Very nice talking to you." Snooky rolled up his window. He waited while she teetered away. Then he floored the accelerator and roared past her, turning the car to block the road. It was a narrow road, and to get past him she would have to go into the woods. The woman stopped, wavering uncertainly on her spike heels. He opened the door and got out.

"It's no good," he said. "I know who you are."

She stared at him, her mouth a red clown circle in the artificial whiteness of her face.

"You're Bobby Fuller's mysterious girlfriend."

Her mouth opened wider, an astonished zero.

"You're on your way to confront Irma Ditmar, aren't you? For stealing Bobby away from you?"

At this she suddenly came to life. "I don't know what you're talking about!" she snapped. She hurried back down the road the way she had come. Snooky, guessing that she had walked all the way from the Lyle train station, a distance of three miles, was impressed by the speed she still managed to muster. He put his hands in his pockets and strolled after her.

"It's no good," he called. "The police know who you are. You and Bobby were seen together. It's only a matter of time until they find you."

"Get lost, creep!" But somehow the ritual words had lost their punch. She teetered wildly on for a few more steps. All at once the bravado went out of her. She got tangled up in her own heels, tripped over herself and fell flat on the rocky road. When Snooky reached her, she was lying there, weeping pathetically.

"Don't cry," he said, genuinely concerned. "Don't cry. Here. Come here."

He helped her over to the side of the road, where she collapsed limply on a large rock. She flailed at him weakly with her hands. "Keep away from me. *Creep.*"

But it was said without real conviction. She opened up her purse and rummaged around, producing a large wad of Kleenex. She peeled one off the top and applied it delicately to her nose and eyes. "My makeup," she wailed. "It's *ruined.*"

Snooky sat down nearby and pulled his coat around him.

It was a pale winter's day, and the sunlight slanted weakly through the trees. "It's cold. You should button up your coat."

"Oh." She scrabbled at it ineffectually, then blew her nose. "Yes."

Now that Snooky had found her, there seemed to be, strangely enough, little to say. She fit Charlotte's description exactly. At the moment, however, with her mascara running and her nose all red, she did not seem terribly brazen. The fight seemed to have gone out of her.

He waited until she had stopped snuffling. "Listen to me," he said in a tone of authority. "You're going to get into my car, and you're going to come with me, and we'll go somewhere in town and talk. The police know all about you. As I said, it's only a matter of time before they catch up with you. I recognized you, didn't I? So you see. I knew Bobby, too. I'll help you if I can, but only if you tell me what's going on. You were on your way to Hugo's Folly?"

She nodded.

"All right. Come with me. I know someplace we can talk. I'll get you something to eat, too. Your feet must be killing you."

"I'm okay."

But Snooky could see tiny spots of blood through her white stockings. She looked down at them, and tears welled up in her eyes. "Damn. Ruined my stockings, too. And these were a brand new pair."

"Come on."

He helped her hobble over to the car. He got in, started the engine, turned the car around and headed down the road in the direction of Lyle. His passenger did not seem to feel like talking. She sat slumped in her seat, staring dully out the side window.

"My name is Snooky Randolph. What's yours?"

"What's it to you?" she snapped, some of the old fighting spirit reviving. Snooky shrugged.

"Don't tell me, if you don't want to. Suit yourself. It

won't make any difference to the police. They have your full description. You and Bobby were seen together in Wolfingham, and you know what a fine police force they have."

She apparently did not know, because this news seemed to depress her. She slumped farther down into her seat, and dabbed at her face with the tissue.

"So what's your name?"

"Diane," she muttered at last.

"All right, Diane. You live around here?"

She turned her face away.

Snooky was wondering where to take her. He drove cautiously down the main street in Lyle. There was really only one choice—Tiny Sam's—but Irma had said she might drop in there later in the afternoon. He checked his watch. He thought they might have time.

When they entered the diner, Diane staggering along on his arm, Tiny Sam's wife looked up from behind the counter and gave Snooky a friendly nod. She gestured toward one of the red vinyl booths in the back. Snooky made sure his companion was comfortably settled.

"You all right?"

"Yeah."

It was so busy that Tiny Sam himself, in addition to a harried-looking waitress, was waiting on tables. He moved ponderously over to the booth and smiled at them. "Afternoon. What can I get for you?"

"I'll have a cheeseburger," said Snooky. "And fries, and a chocolate milkshake. I love your chocolate milkshakes, Tiny Sam."

Tiny Sam smiled. "And the lady?"

"The same, please."

Tiny Sam left, moving like a vast ocean liner through the crowded waters of his diner, the waitress scurrying around him like a miniature tug. Snooky's companion said, "Mind if I smoke?"

"Not at all."

She rummaged in her handbag, drew out a packet of cigarettes, lit one and leaned back with a sigh against the back of the booth. Smoke curled languorously past her face. Snooky could see that underneath the streaked makeup was a pretty, good-natured, rather stupid face, chubby and round, younger than she first appeared. She regarded him suspiciously out of the corner of her eye. "You really know the police?"

"The detective in charge of this case is a close personal acquaintance."

"Really?"

"Uh-huh."

She chewed her lip. "They know about me, huh?"

"Yes, they do."

She sighed and flicked her ash into the ashtray. "I guess I always knew they'd find out about me. You can't hide forever. Some poet said that."

"So true."

"I read poetry myself. I love T. S. Eliot. Don't you? Have you ever read him? I love that bit about 'a pair of ragged claws / Scuttling across the floors of silent seas.' Isn't that beautiful? I guess that describes how I feel right now. A pair of ragged claws, all alone, scuttling across the floors of silent seas."

The effect of hearing T. S. Eliot—and one of his own favorite passages—quoted from the red, overpainted mouth of this grotesque-looking woman was startling. Snooky stared at her.

"You read T. S. Eliot?"

"Yeah."

The meal arrived. Diane dissected her cheeseburger neatly with her knife and fork, eating it in rapid, tiny bites. "Bobby and I used to read poetry together. He had never read T. S. Eliot. I used to read *The Love Song of J. Alfred Prufrock* to him at night." She fell silent, depressed by this memory.

"How did you meet him?"

She regarded him warily. "Why should I tell you anything?"

"Because I'm trying to help you. And because, if Detective Bentley gets hold of you, you're going to need a friend. I speak from personal experience."

The story that emerged, in bits and snatches, helped along by Snooky's questions, was straightforward. Diane—her last name was Caldwell—worked as a hairdresser and manicurist in a shop in Wolfingham. One day, half a year ago, Bobby had walked in for a haircut.

"We started talking—of course I always talk to the customers—and at the end he asked me out. We went out to dinner and talked and talked and talked. Bobby was so . . . so *sensitive*." A large tear glimmered in one mascara-smeared eye. "He was the nicest man I ever met. The kindest. He was always thinking of me, not of himself. We saw each other practically every day for three months. And then he met that—that *woman*."

"And what happened?"

She picked up her smoldering cigarette and inhaled on it vigorously. "I don't know."

"What do you mean, you don't know?"

"He said that that old hag had fallen for him—of course, who wouldn't? She chased after him for a while. He used to come and tell me about it, and we'd laugh together. But then . . . I don't know. Suddenly it wasn't so funny anymore. Bobby started coming to my place less and less, and he always seemed so—so secretive about it. Like he didn't want anyone to know. And we went out less and less, in case anybody might see us. Still, I couldn't believe he'd leave me for that old hag. That *bitch*."

"But he did."

She looked at him forlornly. "Yeah."

"I'm sorry. Did he tell you they had gotten engaged?"

"Yeah. He said it was her idea, not his, but I knew he was lying. He said he still loved me, but I guess he loved her money more. That's what it was—her money. He couldn't resist it. I'm poor, and he was poor, and he always wanted to be rich. I thought it was enough that we were . . . that we loved each other." She began to sob.

"Now, now," said Snooky awkwardly, patting her shoulder. "Here. Have a Kleenex."

"Thanks. I'm sorry . . . I'm sorry. I know I look awful."

"You look much better without all that stuff on your face. Honestly, you do."

"Oh, no, no, no. I hate the way I look. I try not to look in the mirror in the morning when I put my makeup on."

Snooky felt that that explained a great deal about her appearance, but he did not say anything. "When's the last time—I'm sorry, but when's the last time you saw Bobby?"

"The night he got engaged. He drove to my place and told me about it. I couldn't believe it. We had an awful fight." Her eyes filled with tears. "I screamed at him—crazy stuff—I don't know what I said. And he told me he still loved me. But I knew he was lying. He wanted to marry her, for her money. Her *money!* And then a few days later he was dead." She regarded Snooky defiantly. "I found out on the morning news."

"I'm so sorry."

"Yeah. It's okay. He got what he deserved."

"Do you have any idea who killed him?"

"Yeah." She blinked at him. "He told me who did it."

"What?"

"Oh, well . . . what I mean is, he told me all along that if anything happened to him, one of Irma's relatives would be to blame. He used to joke about it, but it made him nervous, I know. He told me they all hated him for coming in and taking away her money. They were afraid she'd leave him everything when she died. So he used to joke about somebody killing him before that could happen. And then—well, then somebody did."

Snooky was silent.

"I wouldn't be surprised if they were all in on it, sort of a family pact." Diane blew out a gust of smoke. "It's a lot of money, isn't it?"

"Yes . . . yes. It's a lot of money. It's an awful lot of money."

"That's what Bobby told me."

"Did he mention anyone—any of Irma's relatives in particular? Anyone who he thought hated him more than the rest?"

She thought this over for a minute. "Well, that guy, what's his name, Irma's brother . . ."

"Roger?"

"Yeah. Bobby thought he was crazy, with his guns and hunting and so on. I think he made him a little nervous. He always hated hunters. Bobby, I mean. He was on the side of the deer." She sighed. "And he never liked that fat woman, either."

"Gertie? Irma's sister-in-law?"

"Yeah, that's the one. She gave him the creeps. He used to say there was something a little funny there."

"A little funny? What did he mean?"

"I don't know." She shrugged. "I didn't care. All I was interested in hearing about was *her*."

"Irma?"

"Yeah."

There was a pause. "So what did you do when Bobby died?"

She lit another cigarette. "I didn't know what to do. I didn't know whether to go to the police, or what. I figured they'd come after me pretty soon, anyway. I knew I was in trouble—jilted girlfriend and all that. They'd pin it on me. So I stayed home from work for a while, and waited it out. But nothing happened—*nothing!* And finally I realized that nobody—nobody at all—knew about me. I had talked to the girls at work about Bobby, but I never told them his last name. And then he made sure that nobody ever saw us together. So I went back to work, and everything was just as before. Except for me. I couldn't stop thinking about it. And I was sure the police were going to find me some day."

"And you started thinking about Irma."

"Honestly, I couldn't get her out of my mind. I wanted

to know what it was that Bobby saw in her. The more I thought about it, the crazier it made me, until today I took the train over here and found out where her house was. I don't know what I would have done, really. Probably just looked at the house for a while and gone away. Except that I was mad—*really* mad. She had no right to do what she did, taking him away from me."

"But she didn't know about you, did she?"

"Oh, no. Bobby never told her. He said it wasn't her fault, that it was all his fault."

"So she didn't know she was taking him away from anybody."

"I didn't care," said Diane Caldwell defiantly. "I didn't care anymore. I just wanted to get a look at her. I couldn't . . . somehow I couldn't keep myself away."

"I understand that."

"Do you?" She looked at him gratefully.

"Of course."

They sat quietly together for a moment. Tiny Sam, sensing a lull in the conversation, trundled toward them, pad in hand. "Anything else I can get for you folks?" he boomed.

"Two cups of coffee, Sam. And two slices of cherry pie." She gave him a faint smile.

When their dessert came, Snooky leaned forward. "Listen to me, Diane. You have to tell the police what you've just told me. Yes, you do," he said when she shook her head. "You don't have any choice. They'll get it out of you sooner or later. I know the detective in charge of this case, so I'm going to go along with you."

"To the police station?"

"Yes."

"Now?"

"Yes."

She picked miserably at her pie. "I don't know. I don't know."

"It's either now, or when the police come and find you."

She turned her pie over, spilling its red gelatinous contents onto the plate, and slowly peeled the bottom crust off.

"Yeah. That's true. But they'll think *I* did it. You know how it is."

"Listen, Diane. Detective Bentley thinks everybody did it. He thinks my brother-in-law, who only met Bobby once or twice, did it. He thinks I did it, for Christ's sake. He's not positive he himself didn't do it. He doesn't have any evidence against you, and it will look good for you if you come forward to tell him what you know."

"Yeah." She sighed deeply. "Yeah. I guess so. Damn. I knew it would be like this, sooner or later."

"One more word of advice," said Snooky. "Don't try to quote poetry to Detective Bentley. He wouldn't understand. The man does not possess a poetic soul. Now finish up your cherry pie, and we'll be on our way."

Bernard felt pleased. He had taken off his shoes, revealing threadbare socks, and was wiggling his toes in front of the fire. There was a Swiss cheese sandwich on a tray on his lap, along with a glass of milk and a cut-up tomato sprinkled with basil. Snooky had called from somewhere in town, sounding very mysterious and saying he wouldn't be home for dinner. Bernard was, frankly, delighted. This allowed him and Maya to have a quiet meal and an evening together, something he had missed a great deal.

His wife was curled up next to him on the sofa. Misty was slumbering at their feet. Maya was eating her cheese-and-lettuce sandwich with an absorbed, abstracted expression on her face. Bernard knew what it was that was occupying her.

"Got an idea for your next article?"

"Huh? Oh, I think so. Something to do with kiwis."

"Kiwis?"

"You know. Those birds from New Zealand. They're adorable looking. A long bill and all this grayish brown hair. I think my readers might be interested."

"I'm sure they would be," Bernard said kindly. He returned to his sandwich.

"I can't find out much about them while we're here. That library in town doesn't look like it would have much information on kiwis to me."

"That library in town doesn't look like it would have a dictionary."

"I'll have to wait till we get home. I can go into New York City and research it at the public library. They'll have a thousand and one references."

"I don't see why we're not home now," Bernard said fretfully. He moved his feet, and Misty grumbled in her sleep. "I don't see why we're not home. I would like to be home. I don't see why we have to spend our lives babysitting your younger brother. It seems grossly unfair."

Maya stared into the roaring flames. "He needs us now."

"You're wrong, Maya. You're misguided. He doesn't need us. He'd be perfectly happy here by himself. He won't be by himself for long, anyway," Bernard added darkly. "Do you get the feeling we're interfering with his petty little social life?"

"No."

"Well, I do."

"Snooky's always going out with somebody. It's in his nature. He doesn't like to be alone."

Bernard did not care about Snooky's nature. "I don't understand why we're still here. Everything's perfectly safe. Nothing has happened since Bobby died. Even Snooky could probably manage here alone."

Maya simply shook her head.

"I'm sure our house has been robbed," Bernard said in gloomy tones. He took a large bite of his sandwich.

"Mr. Sanders said he would look after it." Mr. Sanders lived next door in a large glass-and-wood geodesic dome. Bernard, who loathed the modern style, had almost refused to move into the neighborhood because of Mr. Sanders's house.

"Mr. Sanders was born in the twilight years of the last century. He can't even look after his own place."

"He promised me he would drop by occasionally and make sure everything was okay. He has our number here in case anything goes wrong."

"Mr. Sanders has never 'dropped by' anywhere. He can barely hobble downstairs. I think we should go home and make sure everything is all right. I think it's our civic duty."

Maya and Bernard lived in an old white Victorian with eggshell-blue trim which they had renovated themselves, at great expense. This house was Bernard's retreat from the world, his fiefdom, his private universe. Some of his happiest moments had been spent safely closeted away in his study within the heart of the house, far from the ring of the telephone and the intrusive visits of neighbors.

Maya leaned back luxuriously and closed her eyes. The heat was making her drowsy. She spread her hair out over the back of the sofa, where the firelight gleamed on it, turning it into a deep dark chestnut. "I wouldn't worry, Bernard. I'm sure the house is okay."

"Robbed, I imagine. Robbed. Pillaged and plundered. Burned to the ground. All the plants in the sun room torn down, all our nice furniture carted away. A gang of marauding hoodlums could empty the house in front of Mr. Sanders's nose and he wouldn't see or hear anything."

"That's not true."

Bernard finished his sandwich in a state of deep gloom. "You know what's happened to us, Maya? We're trapped here. Snooky has trapped us here, in the wilderness. We can't leave now. We'll never be able to leave. He's cast some kind of weird spell over us."

Maya put an arm around him. "We'll go home soon, Bernard, I promise. I know you can't stand to be away from home for too long. You're like a bear, just the way Snooky says—you like to hibernate during the winter."

"Would you like some coffee?"

"Mmmm, yes. That would be great."

Bernard heaved himself to his feet and moved off toward the kitchen. He came back ten minutes later with two steaming mugs and a pitcher of cream. He served both of them, then put his arm around Maya. "This is nice."

"Very nice."

"Has it ever occurred to you that Snooky is interfering with *our* social life?"

"We'll go home soon, I promise you." She snuggled up next to him and put her head on his shoulder.

"Okay."

They drank their coffee slowly, savoring it—Snooky always had plenty of excellent coffee beans in the kitchen pantry—then Maya closed her eyes and fell asleep. Bernard stared into the fire until his head began to swim. An hour later, when the door opened, the two of them were huddled together on the sofa, deep in slumber.

Snooky came in, shrugged off his coat and slowly unwound his long red muffler. He sat down opposite them and stretched out his legs toward the fire.

"Touching. Very touching. So these are the joys of marriage. Long evenings by the hearth, alone together, enjoying each other's company."

Maya woke up, yawned, stretched like a sleepy cat, and smiled at her brother. "And how was your evening, Snooks? Fun and games?"

"Fun and games as always, My."

"Please don't tell us about it," said Bernard.

"Really? Now, I think you might be interested."

"Why would we be interested?"

"Because I met someone."

"You're always meeting someone," said Maya. "It's your great personal gift. It's that charming smile of yours and your devil-may-care attitude. Only those of us close to you know how sorely troubled you are underneath."

"I'm not sorely troubled. I'm happy all the way through. You know that, My. So the two of you aren't interested in who I met?"

"It must be a girl."

"Yes."

Maya looked faintly disapproving. "You already have a girlfriend, Snooks. Remember her?"

"This is not a girlfriend, Maya. At least not mine."

Maya arched an eyebrow. "Whose, then?"

"Bobby Fuller's."

Snooky was gratified by the expressions of incredulity on their faces. Bernard sat up straighter.

"You're kidding," he said.

"No, I'm not."

"Bobby Fuller's secret girlfriend?"

"The very same."

"How did you find her?"

"She was marching up the road toward Hugo's Folly, and I recognized her from Charlotte's description. 'Hussy,' by the way, is physically accurate but not strictly fair. She's a very nice person."

"She was going to see Irma?"

"Yes. I stopped, turned her around, took her out for dinner, and we talked. Then I took her to the police station, and Bentley interviewed her. A little while ago I took her home. She lives in Wolfingham, by the way. A nice little studio apartment. She's a hairdresser."

"What's her name?"

"Diane. Diane Caldwell."

"What's her story?"

Snooky related it to him, in detail. When he was done, Bernard said, "Tell me again."

"What?"

"Tell me again."

"Tell you what?"

"Everything she said, Snooky. Tell me again."

Snooky looked reproachful. "But I already told you. Didn't I, My? Didn't I just tell him everything?"

"Do as he says, Snooky."

Grudgingly, Snooky repeated the conversation. Bernard

sat with his eyes closed, his head turned away. When Snooky was finished, he turned to his sister and said,

"Is he asleep?"

"He's listening, Snooks."

"The way he's breathing, I thought he was asleep."

Bernard's eyes opened. "So Bobby felt nervous around Roger and Gertie? Those two in particular?"

"That's what she said."

"Either one of them more than the other?"

"She didn't know. She said Bobby thought Roger's interest in guns and hunting was creepy."

"How about the other relatives—Dwayne and Sarah?"

"She didn't mention them."

"Hmmmm." Bernard lapsed into a thoughtful silence. The flames roared and crackled. The wind gusted outside, rattling the window panes.

Snooky yawned. "I'm turning in, Maya. It's been a long day. Do you know that she quoted my favorite passage from *The Love Song of J. Alfred Prufrock*?"

" 'Ragged claws / Scuttling across the floors of silent seas'?"

Snooky was impressed. "I didn't think you knew me that well, My."

"You're an open book to me, Snooky. William and I raised you from childhood, remember?"

"I'm touched. I'm really touched. I didn't think you knew my favorite line of poetry."

"I know a lot of things about you, Snooks. Not all as benign as *The Love Song of J. Alfred Prufrock*."

"Really? What's my favorite color?"

"Green."

"No. Yellow. You're close, though. What's my favorite piece of music?"

" 'My Hat, It Has Three Corners'?"

"No. Brahms's Piano Concerto Number One in D Minor. Close enough."

Maya looked disgruntled. "It used to be 'My Hat, It Has

Three Corners.' I remember because I had to sing you to sleep with it about a trillion times when you were little."

"That was a long time ago, My."

"Yes." She grew reflective, looking at her brother, his lanky form stretched out on the sofa. "Yes, I guess it was. Brahms's Piano Concerto Number One, you say?"

"Uh-huh."

"All right. Good night, Snooky. Sleep well."

"You, too."

The next day, Bernard seemed distracted. He hummed to himself, grunted as he worked, and spent long hours staring out the window. He corraled Snooky and made him repeat the conversation with Bobby's secret girlfriend again.

"I don't want to talk about it anymore, Bernard. I'm sorry that I found her. I've already told you twice."

"Tell me again."

"No."

"Tell me again."

When Snooky was finished, he began to edge away.

"Wait just one minute," said Bernard. "Where are you going?"

"I have to do the shopping, remember? None of us will eat tonight if I don't get to Harry's before it closes."

Bernard waved him away with a magisterial gesture. "All right. You can go."

" 'You can go,' " Snooky repeated incredulously to his sister later on that afternoon, when he had returned with his arms full of groceries. " 'You can go.' Just like that. Like a . . . a royal command. As if he didn't know I was there anymore, once I had served his purpose."

"You have to understand him, Snooks. Bernard can be very imperious when he's deep in thought."

"He can't be deep in thought all the time. And it's not imperious, My. I call it arrogant. I didn't like his tone."

"I apologize for him."

"You don't have to do that," Snooky said, taking the

groceries out of the shopping bags and tossing them onto the kitchen counter. "No, you don't have to do that."

"Maybe you can manipulate him into apologizing to you again."

"It's not worth it. It's simply not worth it. What's he doing now?"

Maya went to the kitchen door. "He's sitting on the sofa and looking out the window."

"Deep in thought," said Snooky bitterly. As an outlet for his feelings, he tore a piece out of the brown paper shopping bag. Rapidly and neatly, with his long white fingers, he folded it into a paper airplane. Following that, in rapid succession, he produced a paper bird, then a fish, then a tiny elephant. Maya watched admiringly.

"You've always been good at origami."

"I enjoy it."

"You haven't lost any of your talent."

"I only do it when I'm angry. It's kind of a release for me."

"I remember when you were eight or nine years old. There was a time when William said he couldn't turn around in the house without stumbling over some of that brightly colored Chinese paper."

"I remember."

"William was worried for a while that you'd turn out to be an artist."

Snooky smiled. "William was wrong."

"He was worried you'd be an artist, and starve, or eat up the family resources. In his worst nightmares he never imagined you'd turn out to do nothing."

She said it with great affection. Snooky grinned. He held up a delicate paper cat, complete with stubby whiskers. "This is for you, Maya. You look like a cat, you know that?"

"Thank you, Snooks."

"And this is for you, too, in memory of the old days."

He took the remaining bag, smoothed it out, worked on it intently for a few minutes, then handed her a huge floppy three-cornered hat. Maya began to laugh.

In the living room, Bernard was gazing vacantly out the window. Thoughts were churning round and round in his head. Finally he shook himself and put a piece of paper in the typewriter. At the top he wrote:

BBYS GRLFRND ("Bobby's girlfriend")
ANGR ("anger")
JLSY ("jealousy")
PSSSSVNSS ("possessiveness")

and

LS ("lies")

He looked thoughtfully at this last word for a long time. He never believed anything that anyone ever told him about themselves. It was a long-established policy, and one that he found consistently useful. People's capacity for self-deception was nearly endless. They would lie or steal—or kill, he mused—to run away from an unpleasant truth about themselves. It was the nature of the human ego, always frightened, always insecure, always ready to defend itself at the smallest slight. The most painful thing for most people was to appear wrong, or humiliated, or foolish.

Now, this woman, Diane Caldwell, had found herself in an extremely foolish position. She was the girlfriend of a man who had left her for a much less attractive, much older woman, simply for the money. Bernard tried to imagine how she must have felt. Humiliated, no doubt. And angry. Very, very angry.

She had told Snooky that she wasn't the one who had murdered Bobby, but that meant nothing. Still, there were other things she had said that Bernard found very interesting. Slowly, thoughtfully, he typed down two names.

RGR
GRTI

Roger and Gertie. Yes, he found it interesting, that Bobby had singled out these two in particular. These two who were always in the woods . . . who always had a good reason for being in the woods . . . these two who were of the older generation and had been waiting for years to inherit Irma's money. Particularly Gertie . . . it was her brother's money, after all. It must have been painful to see it pass out of her hands, years ago.

But which, if either, of them? he wondered.

At the moment that Bernard was slowly and laboriously typing her name down, Gertie was striding through the woods near the cabin, head flung back, nostrils flared, inhaling the chill winter air deeply. Her round flabby cheeks were flushed red with the cold and high blood pressure—she had known about her blood pressure problems for years, but she didn't let that slow her down, certainly not—and her hair, dyed a peculiar shade of steel blue, bobbed gently around her face. Her eyes were alert with interest, roving here and there, searching the bracken and the trees for possible specimens. A pair of large binoculars hung around her neck. Every so often she knelt to the ground with a whoop of delight and gathered a twig or piece of moss or other decaying vegetation tenderly into her pocket. It had not snowed recently, but it was gray and drizzling and the ground was wet. Gertie was undisturbed. Piglike, she loved mud. Her baggy pants and oversize coat were covered with it, but she did not even notice. She charged on, and the creatures of the woodland cowered, unseen, before her.

As she went, she breathed heavily, snuffling like a warthog. Recently she had noticed that she could not walk as far as she used to. She stopped every now and again to lean against a tree and catch her breath. So *stupid*, really . . . she never used to have to stop at all, not if she walked for miles and miles. Well, she was getting old, there was no doubt about it. Hugo had passed on years ago; the members of her family were not long-lived. She was resigned to it. She felt in tune with the cycles of the seasons, of the flowers and plants, and of her own life. When her time came she would accept her death, just as the animals and plants do. No use fighting the inevitable.

But until then, she was going to enjoy herself. She picked herself up off the tree trunk and marched on impatiently, proudly. As she went, when she was not too short of breath, she hummed quietly to herself. She was a happy woman, she thought. A happy woman. Of course, what was there to be unhappy about? Everything was working out just fine.

Just fine, she thought, eagerly crushing a brown leaf to her face to catch the elusive, damp scent.

Roger, on this cold winter's afternoon, was doing what he had done nearly every afternoon since his retirement. He was sitting in the easy chair in his living room, watching TV. He was watching the television that Irma had bought for him, in the living room that Irma had furnished for him, in the house that Irma had built for him. Roger did not think about these painful facts anymore. He had accepted long ago that his sister was the successful one, with her wealthy marriage. He still saw himself as unfairly wronged by the vagaries of business. It was not his fault, he would reason when forced to think about it; it was not his fault; he had tried hard. Nobody could have worked harder than he did. It was just a fluke; some people succeeded while others failed. He was one of the ones who had not succeeded.

Now he sat, quite happily, sipping a Coke and watching the *Oprah Winfrey Show.* Oprah's guests today were three people who had been raised as the opposite sex: two men who had been raised as women, and one woman who had been raised as a man. Roger made a sympathetic clucking sound. That was awful, wasn't it? What kind of parents would do that to a child? Nobody seemed to know. The people on the show seemed angry . . . well, no wonder. Roger tried to imagine raising Dwayne as a girl. He shook his head. Why would someone do that? He had never wanted a daughter, anyway. To tell the truth, he had never really wanted a son, or children at all; but when he married Dwayne's mother, the boy had been eight years old, and Roger had had no choice but to accept him. Over the years he had become very fond of him. He was a good boy, even if he couldn't figure out what he wanted to do with his life. He was a good son. Roger couldn't imagine him as a daughter.

His attention drifted back to the television set. These were such sad stories. Roger preferred Oprah's lighter shows, the ones with celebrity interviews and fashion models displaying the latest from Paris. He always watched the fashion shows with an all-absorbing interest, even though the majority of the clothes were for women and he would never dream of dressing the way the male models did, anyway. And the celebrity interviews were wonderful. He remembered one the other day with Arnold Schwarzenegger where Arnold had cracked up the audience by saying . . .

His mind drifted off into pleasant reveries.

Dwayne was downstairs in the basement, which he had converted years ago to a darkroom. While the weather was bad, so cold and rainy, he didn't go out much. He preferred to stay safely indoors and work on his photography. Right now he was developing some pictures he had taken over the last few months. With all the excitement going on in the family, with Bobby's unfortunate death and all, and then Aunt Irma's illness, he hadn't been able to escape into his darkroom as much as he wanted to. It was Dwayne's refuge from the everyday world. Now he worked on, during this long winter afternoon, while outside the rain pattered gently against the bare tree trunks and turned the ground to mud. Dwayne puttered around his basement, happy and absorbed, his face a satanic dull red from the photographic light.

First he developed some prints that he had taken at a farmer's market in upstate New York on a trip several months ago. The hearty-looking women with their piles of pumpkins and winesap apples, the strangely shaped gourds, the sheaves of corn and bushels of tomatoes. He smiled as he looked at the photos. He worked in black and white because it was so much easier to develop, but for pictures like these, he wished he had been able to photograph in color. Particularly the one of that girl who sold the apples . . . he had almost gotten up enough courage to speak to her. Maybe next time. Dwayne was shy in general, and particularly shy around women, but he could ask someone out if he wanted to. That farm girl had had nice eyes, bright and sparkling and friendly. He looked at her picture and smiled. Yes, next time he would ask her out.

After that, he worked on some prints he had shot of a family dinner. There they were, all frozen in time. Irma and Bobby at the head of the table, with eyes only for each other. Dwayne smirked. He was not sorry that Bobby was dead. No, he was not sorry at all. Of course, it was horrible to die like that, but still . . . there was Sarah talking to Roger, her hands moving in an expressive gesture. Gertie was sitting at the foot of the table; she seemed to be concentrating on her food. Dwayne looked at the picture for a long time. This was his family, he thought. He was fond of everyone in it, with the exception of Bobby, who had never really been a member. He was lucky, he realized, hanging the print up to dry. Lots of people hated their families. He thought, considering that he wasn't related by blood to any of them, that he was really very lucky.

He looked at the images of Irma and Bobby again, their faces turned toward each other. Really *very* lucky! he thought in a self-satisfied way.

A few days later, Snooky and Sarah were again sitting in the kitchen of Hugo's Folly, having a companionable cup of tea. They were discussing Dwayne.

"He's just like Roger," Sarah was saying. "He gets these wild ideas, these speculations, and he's always sure he's right. I can't tell you how much money Roger's borrowed from Aunt Irma over the years, and it's gone—all of it. She supports him totally."

"Terrible."

"Yes. And Dwayne's the same way—a head full of dreams. Right now he's positive he's the successor to Ansel Adams, with his black-and-white photography. The only problem is, he doesn't have any talent."

"Are you sure?"

"Yes. He's not any good. And he won't take any suggestions or hints, either. He simply tells me I don't understand photography."

"There's nothing you can do about it, Sarah."

"I know. I feel bad about it, that's all. He's going to have a rude awakening one of these days. Right now he's doing nature photography—scenes and so on. For a while there, he was interested in abstract photos."

"Abstract?"

"Oh, you know." She shrugged. "Angles, edges, corners of things. He used to go into the woods and take pictures of tree bark from up close, half a leaf, a corner of a spiderweb. I thought it was ridiculous, but Gertie loved it and encouraged him. He went to Manhattan and took close-up shots of gravel on the sidewalk. And he used to go to Harry's Market and take black-and-white photos of the produce—you know, piles of apples and grapes and oranges—until Harry told him to get moving, he was blocking the aisle."

"No sympathy for artists," said Snooky.

"No. Harry just wants to sell his stuff. He didn't care for Dwayne taking photos of apple stems or whatever he was doing. God only knows."

"Poor Dwayne. The misunderstood photographer."

"Yes." Sarah dabbled a finger thoughtfully in her milky tea. "The thing is, he's not very smart, but he's such a sweet person. I keep thinking there must be something he would be good at."

"Why? There's nothing I'm good at."

"There's lots of things you can do, Snooky. And you're smart, too. You made a choice not to work. It's different for Dwayne. He can't afford not to."

"Can't he?"

Their eyes met. At that moment the back door, in the laundry room next to the kitchen, swung open with a bang. Somebody stomped in, heavy boots thumping against the floor.

Sarah raised an eyebrow. "Gertie?" she called.

There was no answer from the laundry room, just a lot of huffing and puffing.

"Gertie? Is that you?"

The vast bulk which was Gertie hove abruptly into view. "Of course it's me," she snapped. "Who the hell else would it be? Would somebody please help me with these damned boots?"

"You're back early," said Sarah with a worried frown as Snooky went to help.

Gertie collapsed on an ancient, rickety lawn chair that had come indoors sometime the previous summer, nobody knew exactly how, and taken up permanent abode next to the washing machine. She extended one enormously fat leg. "Yes. Nothing out there today. Decided to come home and get some rest."

"Are you feeling all right?" Sarah gazed at her, concerned. Gertie went outside every day, fair weather or foul, and today was sunny and a bit warmer than it had been. "Are you okay?"

" 'Course I'm all right. Just thought I'd come home and get some of my cataloguing done." Gertie kept scrapbooks and boxes full of her collection of specimens. She lovingly listed them in an encyclopedic volume of notebooks which stretched back, stuffed full of her woodland observations, over thirty years. "I'm falling behind on it."

"Oh. I see."

Snooky pulled, and the left boot came off with a loud squelchy sound. Gertie grunted and extended her other leg. "Thanks. That's better. Leave them out here to dry. The woods are still all wet from that rain the other day." She prodded the muddy boots. "Have to clean these someday. Oh, well. Can always put that kind of thing off. I'll be upstairs if anyone wants me. Not that that's too likely. Where's Irma?"

"She's in her room, taking a nap." Sarah looked at her closely. Gertie's face seemed suspiciously flushed. She was still breathing heavily. "Are you sure you're all right?"

" 'Course I am. Don't fuss. Can't bear when people fuss. I'm fine."

"I wish you wouldn't go outside and push yourself so hard every single day, Gertie. It's not good for you, you know. I worry about you."

"Don't be stupid, girl. I've been going out to the woods every single day since long before you were born."

"I know, I know, but you could get hurt, or fall down, and you'd be out there all alone, with nobody to help you."

"They'd find me. Oh, they'd find me, eventually. They found Bobby, didn't they?" Gertie gave a nasty chuckle.

"Yes, but . . . well, that's different."

"Yes, it is. I'm not going to end up a cadaver in the woods, like Bobby. Not that there are going to be any more murders out there, anyway," she added, wheezing slightly. "It's perfectly safe . . . now."

Snooky regarded her curiously. "How can you be so sure about that?"

"Because I keep my eyes open," was Gertie's stern rejoinder. "Most people don't. I'll be upstairs if anybody asks for me. See you later."

And she moved off, wheezing and panting as she went.

Sarah had her head cocked, listening to the sounds of Gertie's breathing as she went down the hall. "I don't like it," she whispered. "The way she sounds. She has high blood pressure and a heart condition, too, you know. She and Irma. It killed Uncle Hugo, years ago."

"Mmmmph."

"Don't pay any attention to what she says about Bobby.

She's always hinting around about him. She thinks she's so observant, but she doesn't know any more than we do."

"Mmmm. Well, you're probably right. More tea, Sarah?"

Out in the foyer, Gertie puffed her laborious way upstairs. She felt terribly short of breath; that was the real reason why she had come home so early. She had been striding through the woods, chasing down a white-breasted nuthatch with her pair of trusty binoculars, when her heart had suddenly made a funny little skip and a jump, and she had been forced to sit down. Her face had gone all red and hot, and she had felt a little dizzy.

"It's nothing," she told herself now. "Didn't sleep well last night—that's all. I'll be better once I sit down to do some cataloging. There's that goshawk feather I found the other day . . ."

Gertie kept minute descriptions of her finds. The goshawk feather, a long gray fluffy one, was her proudest possession in recent months.

She pulled her bulk painfully upstairs and stood panting on the landing. All she could hear was the sound of her blood pounding and knocking in her ears, like the sound of the surf on a vacation she had taken once, in her long-forgotten youth. Even she had been young once, she thought now, without rancor. Even she had been young. She had taken that trip to the seaside with a young man that her parents had disapproved of. It had all been deliciously illicit and forbidden. They had stayed in a little hotel that had been converted from a lighthouse, in a tiny round room at the very top. In the morning, you could wake up and look out the window and see miles in every direction, out over the rolling expanse of sea. The gulls would come and circle, begging for bread—little beggars! she had thought at the time, amused—in their raucous voices. The young man and she had spent a great deal of time alone in that room, suspended in air and space, suspended in time, alone at the top of the lighthouse, with no company except for the sound of the sea and their own voices. How furious her father had been when she got back. She remembered how he had lectured her, over and over. But it hadn't made any difference. Gertie had always done what she wanted. She had been thinner in those days—not thin, of course, never truly thin, but she thought the present-day anorexic look was ridiculous and unbecoming. She had been plump and buxom and hearty, a young girl with a long braid of thick chestnut hair and bright blue eyes that grew luminous (although she did not know this) in the sea air, in the blue twilight at the top of the lighthouse turned motel. She had always done what she wanted. She was the one who had left the young man, who had told her he wanted to marry her. She no longer remembered why she left him. There must have been a good reason. She had left him, and gone her own way, which she had been following ever since. Thinking about it now, old and fat and monstrous, clinging like a wart to the top of the bannister, her blood thundering solemnly in her ears, Gertie felt no regret. She could not even remember his name. No matter. She had never really loved anyone except Hugo.

Hugo . . . and this house. The house that Hugo had built, how she loved it, even more than she had loved that airy, ethereal spire of a lighthouse. Everything in it was so much *Hugo*. She planned to have it to herself one day, although of course there was no hurry. No hurry at all.

Gradually her blood settled down to a muffled roar in the back of her head. She straightened up, wheezing, and went down the hall to her room, where her catalogs waited. She could hear them calling to her as she went . . . *Gertie . . . Gertie . . . it's been too long, Gertie . . . what about that goshawk feather, Gertie! . . . come to us, Gertie . . .*

Invigorated by the call of the wild, Gertie strode briskly down the hall to her room.

8

"Gertie knows something," Snooky announced to Bernard that afternoon when he returned to the cabin.

Bernard looked interested. He pulled a page out of the typewriter. "What?"

"I don't know, but I know she knows something."

"How do you know?"

Snooky related the conversation in the kitchen of Hugo's Folly.

"I see," said Bernard. He thrummed absently on the typewriter keys. "Interesting."

"Of course, it could be nothing. Just Gertie showing off."

"But you don't think it is."

"No."

"What was Sarah's reaction?"

"She told me afterward that Gertie doesn't know anything, but I thought she looked a little upset."

"Hmmm. Interesting."

"Yes."

"Any way we could find out more?"

"Well, I don't think there's much chance of Gertie opening up her heart to you, Bernard. Or me either, for that matter. She's pretty close-mouthed about things."

"But you're sure she knows something?"

"Uh-huh."

Bernard pondered this for a moment.

"I Ching," volunteered Snooky.

"Excuse me?"

"I Ching. It's a kind of Chinese oracle. You use it with sticks or with pennies. Maybe we should consult it."

Bernard turned away.

"You're so close-minded, Bernard. I had a girlfriend once who consulted the I Ching every day. She swore by it. She used to say that thought was meaningless; intuition was all."

"May I say that I am not in the least interested in the sayings of one of your feather-brained girlfriends?"

"You may," said Snooky, "but if you do, you'll hurt my feelings."

Over dinner that night, Bernard appeared abstracted. He grunted to himself and ate his food mechanically. Misty, at his knee, lifted up one paw to beg for food, but for once he ignored her.

Finally Maya leaned forward and touched his elbow lightly. "What is it, darling?"

"What is what?"

"What's the matter?"

"Oh, nothing. Nothing. Just a few ideas rattling around in my head."

"About your book?"

"No. Not exactly."

Maya turned to her brother, who was staring down at the blue-and-white checked tablecloth. "What about you, Snooks?"

"Huh? Oh, I'm all right. I'm okay. I just have a few things on my mind, that's all."

"Things on your mind?"

"Yes."

"A heavy burden for so light a vehicle," remarked Bernard, reaching for the pepper.

Snooky looked embittered. "I'm thinking about what Gertie said today. I'm worried about her. She didn't look well at all. She said she had come home to do her cataloging, but I don't think that was true. Her face was all red."

"High blood pressure," said Bernard.

"And a heart condition, like Irma. Amazing, with all the activity she gets."

"She could probably go on like that for years."

"I hope you're right."

"I nearly always am."

"Just like Mrs. Woolly," said Snooky pointedly. "One of her more annoying traits."

It was Bernard's turn to look annoyed. "Don't start in on Mrs. Woolly."

"Why not?"

"She happens to be my livelihood."

"That's not my fault. I never wanted you to write about sheep. I don't find sheep particularly appealing."

"What would you rather I wrote about?"

"Well, I've always liked marsupials. Kangaroos, you know. Wallabies. Or how about wombats? Nothing nicer than a wombat. They look like little bears. Or how about an opposum?"

"No."

"Bernard likes sheep," said Maya. "And rats. He likes writing about them."

"But Bernard, they're so boring."

"I don't think so."

"How about lizards?"

"No."

"Spiders?"

"No."

"Birds?"

"No."

"Extinct reptiles?"

Bernard gazed at him with a faint frown. "What?"

"Dinosaurs. Pterodactyls. Triceratops. You know what I mean."

"Oh. No."

"Well, don't say I didn't try to help out."

"I like Mrs. Woolly," said Bernard stiffly.

"Nothing wrong with Mrs. Woolly."

"Apparently you think so."

"I didn't say that."

"You haven't said much of anything, as far as I can tell."

"I like Snooky's idea about lizards," Maya said mildly. "You remember that snake you had when you were a little boy, darling? Why not try a book about snakes? You've always liked them."

"I have not. And that snake hated me. It escaped as soon as it could."

"Escaped?" said Snooky. "Where did it go?"

"Down the drain in the sink in my parents' bathroom. When my mother turned on the water to brush her teeth, it reared up out of the drain into her face."

"You're kidding."

"No, I'm not."

"What happened to her?"

"My father claimed she was never quite the same afterward." Bernard sullenly stabbed at his meat with a fork.

"All of Bernard's pets met some kind of gruesome death," said Maya affectionately. "Every single one of them. It's tragic, really."

"Every single one of them? What happened?"

"Nothing."

"Oh, come on, Bernard."

"I refuse to parade my personal tragedies for the sake of satisfying your idle curiosity," Bernard snapped. He stabbed with increasing fervor at his steak.

"My curiosity isn't idle, Bernard. It's active—extremely active. Now, what happened?"

"A series of hideous and tragic accidents in which you could not possibly be interested."

"But I am interested. I am very interested. I couldn't be more interested."

"Tell him about Piggy," said Maya.

"Piggy?"

"Bernard's dog when he was young. Go ahead, darling, tell him about Piggy."

"Piggy died," Bernard said grudgingly.

"How?"

"A friend of my mother's ran him over in our driveway. He liked to sleep in the driveway in the sun. My parents and most of their friends would check for him before they drove in or out. But one day my mother had an acquaintance over for lunch, and when she was leaving she ran over Piggy."

"How sad, Bernard."

"Thank you."

"The saddest part of it is, she didn't run over him just once," said Maya. "She ran over him five or six times."

"Five or six times?"

"The idiot lost her head," said Bernard. "She ran back and forth over him, and then jumped out of the car and ran into the house screaming and crying." He brooded on this. "Once would have been enough. Piggy was not a very large dog."

"I'm sorry, Bernard. Sorrier than I can say. Did you get another dog?"

"Yes, but it wasn't the same. My other dog wasn't as smart as Piggy. Piggy was special." Bernard put a large lump of butter in his potatoes and mashed it down dispiritedly with his fork.

"What about your other pets?"

"Well, there was an aquarium of tropical fish."

"What happened to them?"

"They bred for a few months, then they all died."

Snooky was thoughtful. "Kind of a metaphor for all life, wouldn't you say, Bernard? First we breed, and then we die."

Bernard forked some of the mashed potatoes into his mouth.

"That's why Bernard is so solicitous about Misty," said Maya, smiling at him. "He's worried she'll go the way of the rest."

"Not Misty," said Snooky. He lifted her up and held her with her little paws dangling in midair. "Not this little old Misty. Nothing's going to happen to her. She's smarter than Piggy was. By the way, Bernard, if Piggy was so very intelligent, why did he go to sleep in the driveway?"

Bernard did not reply. Misty woke up, smiled, and yawned hugely into Snooky's face.

The next morning Bernard roused himself bright and early, crept out of bed without waking Maya, put on a heavy sweater and jeans and thick gray socks and went into the kitchen. He made himself a pot of coffee, poured himself a large mug, added thick cream and four sugars and wandered contentedly into the living room. The sun slanted across the floor, and the fire was still smoldering from the night before. He put on another log and stirred the fire a bit, hoping it would catch, which it didn't. He sat down, shivering, at his typewriter. He took a sip of the coffee, which went down warm and sweet and boiling hot. By the time the others got up he was halfway through his second cup of coffee and typing away madly.

Snooky wandered into the kitchen, yawning, his tattered blue robe trailing after him, and Maya went into the bathroom to take a shower. Bernard paused for a moment to look over what he had done. On the floor by his side, the telephone began to ring.

It rang once, twice, three times. Bernard glanced through what he had written, grunted cheerfully to himself and put it back in the typewriter.

The phone shrilled four times, five times. Bernard began to type.

On the ninth ring, Snooky came out into the living

room and stood looking at the stolid figure of his brother-in-law.

"Forgive me if I'm wrong, but isn't that the phone?"

"Yes."

"That's the phone ringing?"

"Yes."

"That phone there on the floor by your side?"

"Yes."

Snooky sighed. "I see." He picked up the telephone. "Hello? . . . Oh, hello, Sarah . . . I . . . what? What's wrong? Calm down. I . . . *what?*"

He listened intently for a moment.

"I'll be right over," he said, and put down the phone. His face had gone gray.

"What is it?"

"It's Irma. She's in bad shape. She's at the hospital."

"The hospital?"

"An overdose of her heart medication."

Their eyes met.

"A suicide attempt," said Snooky.

Bernard was frowning. He looked severe, like a judge. "Or somebody," he said slowly, "doesn't want to have to wait for their money."

When Snooky arrived at the hospital, Detective Bentley was there, interviewing the family.

"Who found her?" he was saying, pen poised above a notepad. Sarah, Gertie, Dwayne and Roger were huddled in a small, miserable group in the waiting room.

"I did," said Sarah. "Snooky, thank God you're here." Snooky sat down next to her and took her hands in his.

"What time was it?" asked Bentley.

"I don't know. Around seven o'clock this morning, maybe. I came into her room, and she was having trouble breathing. I called an ambulance right away."

"The doctors told me she's suffering from an overdose of

digoxin, her heart medication," said Bentley. "An overdose. Who usually gives her her medicine?"

"I do," said Sarah.

"How often do you administer it?"

"Once a day, in the morning. I gave her her dose yesterday around nine o'clock, just as usual. And I only gave her one of the pills, just the way I always do. Not the whole bottle."

"How many pills were left?"

"I don't know. Maybe half the bottle."

"The bottle was kept—where?"

"On the table next to her bed."

"What kind of a mood has she been in recently?" asked Bentley, scribbling furiously. "Has she been depressed?"

"Yes . . . no. Up and down, ever since Bobby's death. Yesterday was one of her bad days."

"She wasn't feeling well?"

"No. She stayed in bed most of the day."

"Did she see anybody?"

"Just Gertie and me. I brought her her meals."

"Any visitors?"

"No."

"Let me ask you something, Miss Tucker," said the detective. "Who else besides yourself would your aunt take her medication from?"

"Well, I always gave it to her personally. I don't know who else she'd trust. Gertie, I guess. Any of the family."

"Thank you." Bentley strode away, his short legs working like pistons, to have a conference with one of the doctors. Sarah turned and buried her face in Snooky's shirt. "He thinks I did it," she said, her voice muffled.

Snooky said nothing. There seemed to be nothing to say.

"I'm going to her," said Gertie.

Sarah looked up, startled. "Gertie, you can't. They're still working on her."

"Fools," said Gertie. "Doctors, I mean. Fools, the whole lot of them." But she sat back down, her shapeless mass a large toadstool on the bright blue hospital chair.

163

Roger had his head in his hands. He was slumped forward at an awkward angle. "I can't believe it. I can't believe it."

Dwayne was staring across the waiting room with a strangely blank expression on his face. He seemed to Snooky to be calculating something inside his head—the look you get when you're adding numbers, or trying to multiply in your head, and you carry the four, but you've already forgotten what the first number was, six or eight or twelve? He seemed withdrawn to a small, central, inner point, where calculations were being made rapidly and smoothly. At Snooky's side, Sarah buried her face in his shoulder and began to sob.

After that first day, spent mostly in the hospital waiting room, time seemed to slow down for Irma's family. The little white digoxin pills had caused a heart attack. Slow and clocklike, like automatons, dulled by the frightening nearness of death, her relatives went back and forth, back and forth between their houses and the hospital. Their lives were ruled by the clock now: visiting hours from ten to twelve, and again from four till six; home again for dinner; back to the hospital the next day, carrying flowers, candy, cards from neighbors. Only Gertie refused to be ruled by the hospital clock. She would sit for hours, ignoring the rules about visitors, holding her sister-in-law's hand and scrutinizing her intently.

"I never knew they were so devoted," Snooky said to Sarah at one point. "Gertie was there all last night, the nurses told me."

Sarah was exhausted. There were pulsing blue veins in the hollows under her eyes. "Thank God for Gertie," was all she said. "Whenever Irma wakes up, there's somebody there."

Gertie's motives were, even for her, a little obscure. Part of it, she felt, sitting by the bed and clasping Irma's frail hand in her own big comforting one, was the fact that Irma was in many ways her last link to her brother Hugo. Irma had been his wife and the three of them had lived together in that house for many happy years. Also, much as she hated to admit it to herself, the proximity of death fascinated her. She sat and watched the life force ebb slowly from her sister-in-law's body. The process fascinated and amazed her. Just so had she watched a sparrow die, crippled by a fall, its rapid breathing slowing gently to a stop. Once she had tried to feed a baby mole that had been abandoned by its parents, left for lost in the middle of the lawn, and halfway through the feeding of warm milk (Gertie didn't know whether moles liked warm milk, but she thought most babies did, and figured it was worth a try), it had given an odd little hiccup and died right there in her hands. She had never forgotten the experience: the sorrow and the sense of loss. She sat for hours, looking at Irma. This was the last person who had truly known Hugo, and here she was fading before her eyes.

After the first drug-induced heart attack, Irma apparently had another, and another, or so the doctors told Sarah. Sarah did not care; she was dulled to all feeling, overwhelmed, insensate. Her life had become an endless round of meals cooked in a blur for the family at home, and long hours spent at Irma's bedside at the hospital. Most of the time Irma slept; even when she was awake, she did not seem to know where she was. She did, however, get agitated if Gertie was not there. "Gertie," she would call out feebly. "Gertie!" She did not seem to recognize any of the others in the family. This nearly broke poor Roger's heart. He would hover for hours over her bed, watching her face, hoping against hope that when she woke up, she would smile and say his name; but she never did. During her wakeful periods, she would look around feebly and ramble on to herself and cry out for Gertie, never anyone else. She had one or two lucid periods, no more. Once, after a visit, Sarah found Roger in the hallway of the hospital. He was sobbing silently, his face distorted.

"She doesn't know me," he said over and over, burying his great shaggy head on Sarah's shoulder. "She doesn't know me!"

Sarah patted his arm and made soothing sounds, but she felt strangely far away and distant. She felt as if her head was floating far above the rest of her body, eyes averted, looking down scornfully at the chaos below her.

Snooky was there constantly, helping her cook for the family, driving her back and forth from the hospital, his face a study in anxiety. Bernard and Maya came and helped out, cleaning the house, bringing in food. Irma was in the hospital three, four, five days, hours that seemed like days, days that seemed like weeks. There was some muttering among the hospital staff that she might pull through, she might recover and get better; but then she would take a turn for the worse and the doctors would leave her room looking abstracted and vague, as if they had already dismissed her from the rolls of the living. Sarah would watch them as they went down the hallway carrying their official-looking clipboards, with their names printed black on white on tiny tags clipped to their pockets (JOHN FALWORTHY, M.D.; LISA HEPPLER, M.D.), the two small initials after their names somehow qualifying them (she thought with rage) to judge over her aunt's life and death. They would murmur to each other in soft professional sympathy, and their faces would tighten and close up whenever a member of the family (of the *already bereaved*, perhaps they were thinking) approached them. They would say something noncommittal and escape, leaving their questioner stranded in the middle of the hall. Sarah would watch them, hating them for their professional competence and their professional indifference, and at times she would think, confusedly, *This can't go on . . . this can't go on . . . I can't go on like this.*

And then, on the sixth day, Irma passed away quietly in her sleep.

The funeral was very grand. Irma's family did not count pennies in their last farewell to her. She was lowered into the space reserved years ago next to her husband's grave. Nearly the entire village of Lyle attended, all the neighbors and friends and distant acquaintances. Tiny Sam and his wife were there, looking as solemn and unmatched as an elephant and a tsetse fly. Carol Ann Studebaker, who ran Dinah's House of Beauty and had done Irma's hair for years, came looking small and leathery as an anteater's snout, her skin brown and wrinkled from too much sun and too many bleaching creams. (There was no Dinah of Dinah's House of Beauty anymore; the original owner had left her husband and run away on a whim with a traveling Australian farmer whom she had met in a bar in Wolfingham, neither of them ever to be heard from again. Her friend Carol Ann, the aging blonde who took over the shop, often wistfully imagined Dinah and her Crocodile Dundee running a big sheep farm, miles of brown land and dirty white sheep, with lots of kids and farmhands all gathered around the table for dinner, Dinah ladling out the soup from an enormous black pot.) At the funeral Carol Ann held a wistful bunch of daisies, which drooped sadly in her hands as she listened to the service.

Harry from Harry's Market came, with his wife in tow, a heavyset woman who looked more ideally suited to Tiny Sam. The Grunwald sisters came, twittering to each other with ill-concealed pleasure that somebody their age had passed on before them. Frank Vanderwoort came, holding a small bunch of forget-me-not's. Detective Bentley attended, his eyes on the family, his expression somber. Everyone watched as the black casket was lowered into the frozen ground. Nina, the occasional cook from Hugo's Folly, who used to come in and lend a hand when there was company, stood on the edge of the crowd and made loud baaaing noises, like a forlorn sheep. Listening to her got Carol Ann Studebaker from Dinah's House of Beauty thinking again about the Australian back country, with its rolling hills (or was it totally flat? she wondered) and its brown grasses and the hot blue sky. Carol Ann stood by the side of a grave on a cold November's day in northern Vermont, shivering in her wool coat (doubtless made from wool from those very sheep, she thought with pleasure), and imagined the Australian sun, as she always pictured it in her mind, a flat heavy disk against an opaque azure sky, the sunlight beating down with a palpable rage.

Snooky looked around at the assembled mourners. All at once his heart leaped up into his throat. There, on the edge of the crowd, shielded from the family's view by the massive bulk of Tiny Sam, was an incongruous figure, totally shrouded in black, with a black veil and black dress and black coat. However, on the top of its head was a bright blue bow, and shockingly orange shoes peeped out from under the coat. Snooky had seen those shoes before. As the service concluded with several solemn admonitions to the living by the local minister ("let her life be an example . . ."), Snooky whispered to his sister, then threaded his way cautiously through the crowd.

"Hello."

"Hello," said the figure.

"Is this some kind of disguise?"

She lifted up the veil, revealing Diane Caldwell's bright blue, heavily mascaraed eyes. "You told me that somebody had recognized me. I thought I should dress so nobody would know."

"Good idea."

"Thank you. Nice funeral, isn't it? I like it when the minister talks about hell. They never seem to think that whoever's died is going there, but they make you feel sure that everybody else at the funeral is."

"Paying your respects?"

Diane Caldwell shrugged. "Not much love lost between me and Irma. This is the closest I'll ever get to her, though. I'm not sorry she's dead. No, I can't say I'm sorry at all."

"I wouldn't say it so loud. There's a murder investigation pending."

She shrugged again. "Somebody did me a favor. There's no way I could have given her those pills. I've never even been to the house. I told you what Bobby said. Somebody in

1 6 8

that family had it in for him. Somebody wants that money real bad."

"Yes."

"They couldn't even wait for an old woman to die," she said. "They couldn't even wait, could they?"

"No."

"Oh, well." She let the veil drop. "I wanted to get a look at the family. They're just the way Bobby described them. I'd keep an eye on them, if I were you. One of them is a killer."

She winked at him roguishly from behind the black veil.

"One of them is a killer!"

The will was read to the family the next day. It was short and straightforward. The house and its entire contents were left to Gertie absolutely, with an ample income to support her for the rest of her life. The rest of Hugo's fortune was divided among the remaining family members, Roger, Dwayne and Sarah. This meant that all four of the surviving family were extremely wealthy.

Snooky, who was waiting outside the living room for the lawyer to finish, watched their faces carefully as they filed from the room. Sarah looked distant, cold, somehow uninvolved in the proceedings. Gertie, on the other hand, looked positively triumphant. She smiled to herself and fingered the gewgaws on the front table with a proprietary glee. She righted one of the portraits which was hanging askew. Roger, next to her, was in tears. He had started crying when his sister was rushed to the hospital, over a week ago, and he could not seem to stop. He carried a large handkerchief, red with blue checks, and mopped his face continually. Dwayne, as before, looked closed and secretive. The truth was that he was thinking that now he could set up a real photography studio, one in which he could do color prints, and maybe hire somebody to help him. He would never have to worry about supporting himself or borrowing money from his stepfather again. In his mind he was calculating how much it would cost to buy that little old shed he had seen on the edge of town and convert it into a studio, complete with all the latest fixings and gadgets.

"How are you?" Snooky said to Sarah.

"Fine." She looked at him coolly, as if her attention were elsewhere.

"Everything all right?"

"Yes. Fine."

"The house is mine!" screamed out Gertie suddenly, in a high-pitched, hysterical voice. "The house is mine!" She was holding one of Irma's grotesque Victorian knickknacks, a small silver monkey with an inquisitive expression and a bell around its neck. She stared at the rest of the family, who stood silent and shocked around her. Then she broke away and galloped up the stairs to her room. They could hear the door close with a triumphant *bang!* behind her.

"Gertie acted very strangely," reported Snooky that evening. "Very strangely indeed."

Bernard sat silent and attentive as Snooky related what had happened. "Hmmmpphh. Interesting."

"Yes."

"And the will—?"

"Divided equally among all of them, with the house and everything in it left to Gertie."

"I see. That's what was expected?"

"Yes."

"Hmmmm."

Snooky collapsed into a chair and rubbed his head wearily. "I feel exhausted. I feel as though I haven't slept in days."

"You haven't," said Maya, who was sitting at the table surrounded by books from the local library. She was thumbing through a large red book entitled *Exotic Flora and Fauna*.

"Is that true? I haven't slept?"

"Yes."

"Sarah's acting strangely. Sort of detached. I can't seem to get through to her."

Maya looked at her brother with compassion. "Why don't you go and lie down, Snooks? We'll make dinner and bring you something. You deserve to be waited on, after all you've been through. You've practically lived at the hospital for a week now."

"Thanks, My. I think I will."

Snooky left the room. They could hear the old bedstead groan as he flung himself down on it. Bernard said irritably, "I don't like the way this is going. Now we're cooking and cleaning for *him*. I thought we came up here to be his guests."

"Bernard, sweetheart."

"Plus, people are dying again. Every time we see your brother, we end up going to somebody's funeral. He only seems to know people who have just days to live. He really is born to trouble, the way you said."

"Bernard."

"I want you to know I don't like the way this is going," he said ominously, turning back to his typewriter.

"There were only two sets of fingerprints on that bottle of pills," Detective Bentley said to Sarah. "Yours and your aunt's."

Sarah shrugged. "That doesn't prove anything."

They were sitting in the living room of the Folly. Bentley had insisted on coming by and interviewing Sarah and Gertie again, and Sarah had called on Snooky for moral support.

"So you think it was suicide?"

Sarah regarded him remotely, her face impassive. "I don't know."

"Why would she kill herself now?" asked Bentley. "It doesn't make any sense. She was getting better."

"Her health was poor. She was very often depressed."

"You don't think it's far more likely it was murder?"

"I don't know, Detective."

"You don't know," snapped Bentley, rising to his feet.

1 7 1

"You don't know. Nobody knows. Nobody seems to know anything about these deaths. Nothing!"

Sarah did not answer.

Bentley gave a snort and left the room. In the front hall he encountered Gertie, who was edging her way down the stairs, breathing heavily through her nose like a wild boar. Gertie, if the truth be known, was not feeling very well, but it was such a gorgeous day out—one of those brilliant, cold, sun-drenched New England autumn days—that she could not resist. She imagined the goshawk waiting for her, perhaps hiding a tidbit or two in the bole of a tree and feasting on it like a king feasting on golden plates. Just so had she seen it a few weeks ago, having its lunch, its gray feathers hunched with a primitive joy. She edged her way slowly downstairs, clutching her binoculars, her eyes wide with anticipation.

"Miss Ditmar. Just the person I want to see."

She regarded the detective ungraciously. "Well? Make it short. I have a lot to do today."

"Did you ever give any medicine to your sister-in-law?"

"No," she snapped.

"Never?"

"Never."

"Can you think of any reason why she would want to take her life?"

"What a stupid question. Of course I can. Her fiancé was dead and her health was failing. What else do you need?"

"So you think she killed herself?"

"Well, I didn't kill her, if that's what you're asking. Now let me ask you something, Detective."

"Yes?"

"Do you have any proof—any proof at all—that my sister-in-law was murdered?"

Bentley shook his head slowly.

"I thought so," said Gertie cunningly. "In that case, please stop coming around and bothering us. I have to go now. Good-bye."

As Bentley left, Sarah came into the foyer. "Oh, it's you," Gertie said rudely.

"Yes. How are you feeling today, Gertie?"

"Fine. I'm on my way out. Now that that idiot detective has gone."

Sarah thought she did not look well—her color was high and she seemed to be breathing quickly—but she did not say anything. She knew it was pointless to interfere. No force in nature could keep Gertie away from the woods on a day like today. "Well, be careful. Don't overdo."

"Don't be silly. I never overdo. Good for me, all my walking."

Gertie bent over to lace up her boots, which had been thrown carelessly under the hall table. When she straightened up, her face was bright red. She leaned against the banister for a moment and then said abruptly,

"Sarah."

Sarah looked at her inquiringly. "Yes?"

"Something I want to say to you."

Sarah waited, but Gertie seemed to be having difficulty going on. She grunted to herself softly for a moment. "About the house."

"Yes, Gertie?"

"You can stay here as long as you like. No, don't say anything. Didn't want you to think I'd throw you out in the cold or anything like that."

Tears sprang to Sarah's eyes. "Oh, Gertie—"

"Don't say anything. Can't stand when people say things. Wanted you to know how I felt, that's all. You can stay here as long as you like."

She turned and thumped her way down the hall. Sarah heard the back door open and close with a dull bang. She went into the laundry room and watched from the window as Gertie, clothed now in her great gray shapeless mackintosh, with her stubbly boots sticking out underneath it like roots from a tree, crossed the little garden out back. Gertie stood at the edge of the woods for a minute, adjusting her binoculars, looking around her at the bright winter day and inhaling with satisfaction (her color looked a little better now, Sarah noted), before stumping away into the shadow of the trees. For a moment her massive form lingered, huge and gray, against the blue and green shadows. Then she was gone.

"Damn it," said Roger. "Damn it. Damn it, damn it, damn it."

He regarded the detective with a touching air of helplessness. "I mean, *damn* it," he said. "No, I didn't sneak over to the Folly that night and give my sister an overdose of pills. How could you think . . . what kind of person do you think . . . damn it, man, how *could* you?"

Overcome, he sank back into his favorite armchair and gestured with the television remote control.

"I was here, watching TV. I'm always here, watching TV. I'm the original couch potato. Dwayne and I had dinner together that night, like we always do, and then we watched some TV and later on we went to sleep. Neither of us got up in the middle of the night to rush over to the Folly. Isn't that right, Dwayne?"

"Yes, Dad."

Dwayne was crouched against a sofa, watching the detective with distaste. "What makes you think somebody killed her, anyway? Why couldn't it be—you know—"

"Suicide?" said Bentley. He was scribbling on his notepad. "There's a great deal of money involved, Mr. Costa. As you know."

Dwayne flushed. "I don't know what you mean by that," he said hotly. "I never wanted Aunt Irma's money. I never wanted it."

"But you could use it, couldn't you?"

"Well, of course I can use it. Anybody can use *money.* Who doesn't need more money? Of course I can use it. But there's no need to imply—well, what you're implying."

"That you killed your aunt for it?"

Roger leaned forward, his face mottled. "You're out of

line, Detective. Way out of line. Dwayne loved my sister. I loved my sister. Everyone in the family loved her."

"Everyone?"

"Yes."

"Let me ask you something, Mr. Halberstam. You knew your sister. Who would she have accepted pills from, perhaps in a confused state, not realizing how many she had taken?"

"Sarah always gave her her heart medication," Roger said slowly.

"Would she have taken it from anyone else?"

"I don't know. Me, of course. Her own brother. Gertie, maybe. Dwayne. I don't know."

The little detective sat and looked at the pair of them, the older man and the younger one, for a long time. "Interesting," he said at last.

"What's so interesting?"

"That nobody in this family seems to know anything."

A few hours later Roger was out in the Folly woods, hunting. He was carrying his Winchester rifle (he had had a funny feeling about it since the day it had been used to kill Bobby, but after all, it was his only gun, and a good one too —it had been *damned* expensive), and looking around for likely victims among the woodland fauna. So far he had been unsuccessful. The truth was that in hunting, as in most things except television watching, Roger was pretty much a failure. He rarely shot at anything, preferring instead to tramp for hours through the woods; and when he did shoot, more often than not he missed. He had bagged very little game for years now. He had tried to teach Dwayne when the boy was young, and Dwayne had picked it up much more easily than he had. So, for that matter, had Irma, who used to enjoy shooting of an afternoon. Nearly everybody shot better than he did, he reflected. But never mind. He enjoyed himself. He supposed Gertie would call what he was doing a "nature walk," but he preferred to call it hunting. Sounded better; more manly, more virile. He strode through the trees, his gun over his shoulder, his eyes alert for game. Really, there was very little difference between what Gertie did and what he did, he mused, in a surprisingly philosophical mood; except that when she saw a small woodland animal, she tried to catalog it, and when he saw one, he tried to shoot it. Basically very little difference.

He tramped the woods happily for several hours, until the afternoon shadows grew long. *These short days*, he thought irritably, and turned back toward home. His route took him through the heart of the Folly woods, to hit the road leading back to town. He had driven halfway up the road and left his old Jeep there, parked on the side. He was not worried about its being stolen; nothing had ever been stolen in Lyle except for Charlotte Grunwald's handbag, years ago in Harry's Market when she foolishly left it lying on top of the apples while she was fingering the string beans. Everybody believed that it was old Mrs. Hickok, who lived on the edge of town and was widely thought to be a witch, who had taken the handbag, less for the money or credit cards than for the sheer satisfaction of spiting poor Charlotte, who had incurred her enmity over some small matter obscured by time. Charlotte had always insisted that it was Mrs. Hickok who filched the handbag, but there was no proof, besides the fact that she had been one of the customers at Harry's at that time, and that she had been seen hurrying down the road toward her little cottage with a gleeful expression on her face. People whispered that she used such articles—clothing, wallets, whatever she could lay her hands on—to put a curse on the unfortunate owner; but there was no proof of that, either. Charlotte had started complaining shortly afterward of pains in her hip, but Roger was sure it was all imaginary. Charlotte always had been a bit of a whiner, perhaps because her sister always demanded —and received—all of the attention. His thoughts drifted off into speculations on how old the Grunwald sisters actually were; they had never revealed their ages, and village speculation ran from their early sixties into their early seventies, with one denizen of Lyle insisting she had it on excellent authority that Alicia was pushing eighty. Roger doubted that. She did not seem that old to him . . .

Out of the corner of his eye, he glimpsed a large shape standing immobile in the shadow of the trees. He peered curiously. Surely there was something there . . . perhaps an animal, trying to hide from him before it bolted? Feeling a sudden shiver of excitement, he hefted his rifle to his shoulder and paced slowly forward.

Yes, there was definitely something there. A large shape hovering behind a boulder; it was difficult to make out exactly what it was, although it did not really look much like a deer . . .

Roger was ten yards away, his face dappled with sunlight, his eyes bulging with the excitement of the kill, when all at once he put his rifle down. He stared and stared.

"Oh, dear Jesus God," he said.

He picked his way slowly through the underbrush until he came to the small clearing where Gertie was sitting, immobile, on a boulder. He did not have to look closely to know she was dead. He, like Gertie, had seen death before, in the shape of small rabbits and squirrels and birds, shot down or found breathing their last on the woodland floor. She sat slumped to one side, her head resting on one outflung arm, leaning against one of the trees she had loved so much.

"Oh, dear Jesus God," said Roger again, in helpless despair. He could not think of what to do. He sat down on a nearby rock and began to sob. This seemed a natural continuation of his mourning for his sister: first Irma, and now Gertie. He did not know what had killed her, but he was sure it was her heart. It had been bad for years. She had sat down to rest, and it had simply given out, thundering to a halt like a regiment of cavalry.

Gertie sat silently watching him from behind her dead eyes while Roger snuffled and blubbered, wiping his streaming nose on his navy blue flannel shirt. It was too much, he

1 7 7

thought, too much, all in such a short time. There was no one to see him except Gertie and the trees, with perhaps a curious squirrel or two, so he let go and gave vent to his feelings. The afternoon shadows grew longer, deepening to violet and black. Finally, he wiped his streaming red face and stood up. Time to go, he thought. Time to go and find somebody to look after poor Gertie.

He saluted her solemnly, lifting his red-checked hunting cap. He had never liked her much, but she had been family, and he had known her for thirty years, since his sister married Hugo. Family. Half his family was gone already, for Christ's sake. Gone. He realized with bitter shock that he was the only one left of his generation. First Hugo, then Irma . . . and now Gertie.

He stood for a moment in the clearing, lifting his cap in a tender salute. "Good-bye, Gertie," he said out loud, to the trees. Then he turned and, finding his gun on the ground, picked it up and walked rapidly away through the darkness.

9

Gertie's funeral was a much more solemn affair than Irma's had been. One death in the family had been vaguely enjoyable to their friends and neighbors, especially with the possible overtones of foul play. Two deaths were widely considered to be in bad taste. This, combined with the family's association with Bobby's death, made the whole thing a bit too much, it was felt. The villagers attended dutifully, but their faces were blank and their voices were muted.

Bernard felt personally insulted by Gertie's death. He had a horror of death, fueled by his childhood images of his great-aunt swinging mistily up and down the stairs; yet somehow his life seemed to have become, as he remarked bitterly, a recurring carnival of funerals.

"Was it natural?" he had asked Snooky when his brother-in-law had come home a few days before, oppressed by the news.

"Natural? Yes, I think so. The doctor said it was a heart attack. She had been failing for a long time—it turns out everybody knew that—but she hated doctors. She never thought there was anything really wrong with her."

"No slow-acting poison, or an overdose of digitalis, or anything like that? Anything to tie it in with Irma's death?"

"No. Not that I know of, Bernard. I'm sorry to disappoint you."

"Somebody could have wanted the house."

Snooky had sat down wearily and rubbed his head, which always ached these days. "I don't know. Not that much. Not enough to murder poor old Gertie. Everyone else in the family has enough money of their own now."

"But the Folly is valuable, isn't it? Who gets it now?"

"I don't know. They're going to search Gertie's room for a will. They're not even sure she made one. It would be like her not to think of it."

Bernard nodded.

Now he stood silently watching as the massive black casket was lowered into the grave on the other side of Hugo's. Gertie had reserved a space for herself by her brother. Irma on one side, and Gertie on the other—the two women who had loved him. The minister spoke a few short words, but even he seemed disoriented by this sudden demand on his services.

Roger, to his own surprise, did not cry during the funeral. He supposed it was because he had been drained dry by his outburst in the clearing. He stood dully watching through bloated eyes as Gertie's casket was lowered into the grave. Who was left? he wondered. Who was left? Just Dwayne and Sarah, his stepson and his niece. Nobody from the old days. Nobody who remembered the past.

He felt suddenly very much alone.

Dwayne, at his side, listened to the service stoically. He felt sorry for poor old Gertie—it was too bad, after all, that somebody who had enjoyed life so much should have been taken away like that, struck down in what could have been her prime—but he had other, more important things to worry about. Dwayne had the kind of mind that could, by and large, block out disturbing events, such as the sudden deaths of two members of his family. For the past few days his mind had been occupied with a new kind of light meter

that he had seen advertised in one of his photography journals, a special kind from Japan (of course, mostly everything
was made in Japan these days), and he was thinking about
ordering one from New York. It was ridiculously expensive,
of course, but that didn't matter anymore. He could afford
to indulge himself. His thoughts drifted away on this happy
note, a clear blue spot in the middle of the dreary winter
day. And perhaps he would get that new tripod as well. Yes,
what an excellent idea. He could use a new one. His old
tripod had a tendency to dip to one side, then curtsey gently
to the ground. It made it difficult to take still pictures if the
tripod wasn't still. Yes, he would get that new tripod, and
the light meter, and maybe that background screen he had
seen in the newest issue that had arrived yesterday . . .

Sarah, next to Dwayne, was saying a silent farewell to
Gertie. She had liked Gertie, who had always been kind to
her, despite the lack of any blood relationship. She was
merely her sister-in-law's niece, yet Gertie had always
treated her like family, welcoming her back gruffly when
Sarah returned from college and took up residence in the
Folly. Irma and Gertie had raised her after her parents died.
Now both of them were dead. She felt tears welling in her
eyes. Who was left? Just Roger and Dwayne. She looked at
what remained of her family critically. She had never felt
very close to either of them. She disapproved of their lacka-
daisical lifestyles. And now Dwayne was talking about
making a living doing his photography full time! She shook
her head mentally. It was lucky he wouldn't ever have to
support himself. Her thoughts, like Dwayne's, drifted
slowly away from the funeral service, rising and mixing
with the clouds in the impassive gray sky. That was a very
generous will that Aunt Irma had made . . . she wondered
who Gertie had left the Folly to . . . maybe one of her
many conservation societies that she corresponded with so
enthusiastically by mail. It was time for Sarah to move on
as well. She'd stay here until the fall, then go to whatever
law school accepted her. Let Roger and Dwayne spend the
rest of their lives here; she had better things to do. Unlike

them, she had ambitions, and the fantastically lucky stroke of being suddenly wealthy hadn't changed that at all . . .

The minister was talking about Gertie's love of the outdoors and compassion for all living things. All the villagers were nodding sagely, even those who during her lifetime had thought Gertie was half-cracked and a bloody nuisance, roaming the woods like that every day. Afterward, the congregation thronged around the family, murmuring their condolences, a stream of earnest sympathy. The Grunwald sisters lingered for a moment, Charlotte with her hand timorously placed on Roger's arm, as if to reassure herself that he was still among the living.

At last the family was left standing alone on the hilltop, with the lowering clouds all about, reaching down in tendrils of mist toward the rocky ground. Maya and Bernard said a muted farewell. Snooky wanted to go with Sarah back to the house, but she refused.

"No, Snooky. I need to be alone with Roger and Dwayne now."

"All right. I understand. I'll call you later."

He stood on the hillside and watched as the three forlorn figures straggled slowly down the hill in the direction of the Folly.

Bernard came home, sat down in front of the fireplace and announced to no one in particular, "I hate funerals." He took off his jacket and tossed it aside, then tore savagely at his tie, which he had knotted uncomfortably tight.

"That's no surprise," said Snooky. "You hate weddings, too. And parties. You hate anything that involves more than one other person."

"I hate staying here with you."

Snooky was not miffed. "A troglodyte," he said pleasantly, taking off his own jacket and laying it on top of Bernard's. "That's what you are, you know. A troglodyte. A primitive cave dweller. An antisocial recluse. You would have been perfectly happy in the days before fire. Living in a cave with a few other people, going out to hunt for food, coming back at night, speaking in monosyllabic grunts, occasionally waging war with cave dwellers from other caves. That life would have suited you perfectly."

"I don't think so."

"Yes, it would."

"I would not have waged war."

"You wage war now with society. As far as you're concerned, you and Maya live alone in a cave in Connecticut, and everyone else is an outsider."

Dinner that night was a subdued affair. The three of them were lost in their own thoughts. The fat blue candle had burned low on the table before Snooky came to with a start and muttered something about cleaning up the dishes. He stacked them with a clatter and went into the kitchen with Maya.

Bernard got up, stretched pleasantly, and heaved himself over to sit down on the sofa. He thought perhaps he could get some work done, for once. Surely nobody else would be inconsiderate enough to die any time in the immediate future, disrupting his work once more with this unrelenting round of hospitals, funerals and condolence calls. He put a sheet of paper in the typewriter, pulled the rickety stand closer to him, and settled down for the evening.

He worked happily for a while, the back of his mind soothed by the splashing noises and snatches of song coming from the kitchen, where Snooky was doing the dishes. Snooky often sang while he did the dishes. It was a pleasant sound, a light tenor that blended harmoniously with the sound of rattling dishes and running water. Unfortunately, Snooky sang only the songs he knew best, the ones that stuck in his head, which right now meant a medley of radio jingles.

A short while later Bernard ran into a snag. Mrs. Woolly was being difficult again. She had just taken a little boy by the ear and was dragging him down to the stream to wash behind his neck. He was screaming, and the other children were ashen-faced. This was unusual violence for one of Bernard's books, and he couldn't understand how it had crept

1 8 3

in, except that all of these recent deaths had made him angry. He also had a memory of himself as a little boy, held by his great-aunt by the ear and forced to wash in exactly the same way; except that it wasn't a stream, it was the big old washtub in the kitchen that he was dunked into headfirst. He crossed out the section with a fat red pencil and began over again. Mrs. Woolly was telling a story . . .

An hour later he sat back and looked thoughtfully at the small pile of pages. Not bad. At his feet, Misty whined and lifted up her head to be scratched, craving a little attention. While Bernard worked, very little else existed for him.

He scratched Misty's head and read over what he had done. This was better. Mrs. Woolly was safely back in her role of kindly leader. Bernard put it back on the pile, then picked up Misty and stroked her back. He looked at the fire, his thoughts drifting away from Mrs. Woolly. Snooky had said he often saw images in the fire, people and places and things from the past and the future. Bernard let his vision blur into a contented rosy haze, golden sparks leaping in the background. His thoughts drifted back to his home in Connecticut . . . he and Maya at Sunday brunch, sitting around their mahogany table, drinking coffee and doing the crossword puzzle . . . the two of them watching TV on a long winter's evening . . . himself alone in his little study, at his massive wooden desk, working away for hours, undisturbed by the telephone or by callers, confident in the knowledge that Maya was guarding the door from all intruders . . . he and Maya alone, going about their lives, responsible to nobody but themselves. Bernard's heart ached. How he longed to be home again. He felt like an exile in this strange, cold, northern land, with its brittle sunshine and its spiky, desolate woods. If only the police could unravel the truth behind these deaths, then maybe—just maybe—Snooky would let them go. Bernard knew his wife; she would not want to leave until the investigation had been thoroughly wrapped up. And now, with the recent spate of deaths, the situation had become even more difficult.

His mind drifted away on a gentle stream of speculation. Gertie . . . Irma . . . both dead now . . . Sarah, with her red hair, so much like Misty's . . . Roger . . . Dwayne, a loser if ever Bernard had seen one . . . now, wasn't there something Snooky had mentioned . . . something he had said recently, something a little odd . . . ?

A few minutes later, when Maya and Snooky came out of the kitchen, they found Bernard sound asleep. His head was resting against the back of the sofa, his face was bathed in firelight, and his mouth was wide open. Misty, on his lap, was snoring.

"This is nice," said Snooky. "I like to see a man working hard."

"Sssshhh. You'll wake him."

"It's only ten o'clock."

"He's had a hard day. He really does hate funerals."

"Who loves them?" Snooky asked reasonably.

"I'll wake him up in a little while and help him to bed. It's peaceful here, Snooky." Maya stretched out her long legs onto the coffee table, and dabbled a finger in her cup of hot chocolate. "Very peaceful. You know how to create an environment."

"Thank you."

"You should be a host more often, instead of a guest. Your considerable talents are wasted as a guest."

"No, Maya. No. I fear that you are wrong. I am also the perfect guest. Anyone who can stay with Bernard for more than two days has to be the perfect guest, someone highly skilled in the art of imposing on people."

"You are that."

"Thank you."

In the middle of the night, Bernard sat up with a start. Where was he? Oh . . . right. He had somehow, in a befuddled daze of sleep, managed to throw off his clothes and climb into bed. He remembered getting up off the couch at Maya's urging and staggering toward the bedroom. After that, oblivion had come quickly.

His mind was racing. He pulled up the pillows, hunching them behind his head. Yes . . . yes . . . that was it, all right. He had it!

His heart began to beat loudly, so loudly that he thought Maya could hear it and would awaken and tell him to go back to sleep. He could see the outline of her cheek in the moonlight, her dark hair falling over her face, her chest slowly rising and falling to her peaceful breathing. She did not seem aware of his heart. She was buried in her dreams. After a moment, he moved aside the thick covers and got stealthily out of bed.

He put on slippers and a robe and, closing his bedroom door silently behind him, padded down the hallway to Snooky's room. The fire had burned low and the cabin was freezing. He shivered miserably in his thin robe. Opening Snooky's door, he crept inside.

Snooky's window was wide open, the curtains flung back to let in the pale blue streaks of moonlight. The room was at least thirty degrees colder than the rest of the cabin. Snooky was sprawled across the bed, his head hanging off the side, one arm flung over the edge, the covers mangled in a pile on top of him. He had a pillow scrunched over his face and another one behind his back. He barely seemed to be breathing. Bernard minced unhappily across the cold floor. He shook his brother-in-law's arm.

"Snooky—Snooky!"

Nothing happened. Snooky's chest, Bernard noticed in a detached manner, was fluttering gently up and down. He seemed to be comfortable in this unorthodox sleeping position. The moonlight streamed in, outlining his rangy form under the pile of twisted blankets.

Bernard wobbled his arm again. "Snooky!"

The pillows moved, the blankets moved, and the arm moved. The pillow slipped aside, and an eye regarded him reproachfully from near the floor.

"Bernard?"

"Yes?"

"Is that you?"

"Yes."

"I'm asleep. I assume you didn't notice?"

"I have to talk to you, Snooky."

"Talk to me?"

"That's right."

"Now?"

"Yes."

The eye regarded him more reproachfully than ever. Snooky heaved himself up on the bed, switched on the bedside light, grabbed the pillows and adjusted them behind him.

"Of course," he said. "Sit down. Please. So you have to talk to me now? God knows you never want to say a word to me when the sun is up. Have a seat."

Bernard sat down on the edge of the bed. "I have to talk to you," he repeated woodenly.

"Of course you do. It's—" Snooky checked the clock on the stand by his bed, "it's four o'clock in the morning. I'm pleased, actually. I was hoping someone would come and engage me in conversation right around now."

"It's about Bobby's murder."

Snooky's eyes narrowed with interest. "Yes?"

"I don't know who killed him."

"Neither do I. Thank you for waking me up to tell me that."

"But I think I know how to find out."

"How?"

Bernard told him.

In the darkness, Snooky's face shone with a ghostly pattern of light and shadows, like a clown's face inexpertly applied. "You're right," he said slowly. "You're absolutely right. That's what she was hinting about. Damn it. Why didn't I see that?"

"You've had a few other things on your mind."

"We'll have to go over to Hugo's Folly first thing in the morning. I'll find out when Sarah's not going to be there."

"Good. Are the police still sniffing around at the Folly?"

"Not that I know of. Bentley has talked to everyone several times, and he doesn't seem to be getting anywhere. This case has him confused."

"It has everybody confused. One more question, Snooky. Why is your window wide open?"

"Fresh air," said Snooky. "Fresh air, Bernard. Wild air. Raw, natural air. Air as it was meant to be. It's good for you."

"I see. Good night."

"Good night."

After Bernard had left, shuffling away on frozen feet, Snooky switched off the light and sat for a long time looking out the window. The moon had sunk low and could be clearly seen, its brilliant white orb surrounded by witch's clouds. A branch from the great oak tree outside the cabin scratched forlornly on the glass, making a distant creaking sound, like someone trying to communicate in an alien language. Usually Snooky found the oak tree's speech reassuring, but now it seemed vaguely ominous. He felt the skin on the back of his neck prickle. He knew himself well enough to know that sleep would be elusive for the rest of the night. He threw aside the covers and went barefoot out to the kitchen, where he made himself a cup of boiling hot milk and honey. Carrying it back to his room, he climbed into bed and huddled comfortably underneath the quilt, cradling the mug in his hands and breathing in the sweet hot vapor gratefully. His mind was racing. Sarah . . . Gertie . . . he hoped very much that Bobby's murderer would turn out to be Gertie, as she was dead already and the knowledge could not touch her. Roger . . . Dwayne . . . well, perhaps it was Roger, with his gun and his hunting habits. Although God knows Sarah had said he couldn't hit an elephant at a distance of three paces. Apparently he never hit anything. He just talked a big show.

Snooky sighed, his head drooping. The milk drink made a warm soft spot in his stomach. He lay down, burying his head under the pillows. Fifteen minutes later he was sound asleep, sprawled in his favorite position crossways on the bed, the blankets twisted around his legs.

The next morning, Snooky's little red car crunched up the long gravel driveway to the Folly. Snooky and Bernard got out.

"You're sure Sarah's not here?"

"Positive. She said she'd be out all morning."

Snooky opened the door, which was, as always, unlocked. They went into the foyer, where the mirrors and brightly polished gewgaws winkled solemnly at them. He led the way upstairs and down the long hallway to Gertie's bedroom.

The room was as neat and clean, as rigidly organized, as it had been when its denizen was alive. Gertie had been scrupulous about keeping her nest clean. There was a small bed with brass knobs on the corners, one narrow window, a long wall taken up entirely by bookshelves, and an antique desk, piled high with papers and books. Gertie's collection of woodland specimens was proudly displayed on several shelves, the trophies of thirty years of forest scavenging. Snooky moved over to the bookcase. Nearly all the books were nature directories and encyclopedias, thick red books with titles like *Wildlife of North America* and *Wildflowers of New England.* They were arranged, with Gertie's meticulous sense of order, by subject and by size. On another shelf were several rows of paperback books, again organized by size. Bernard knelt down to look through them. They were mainly children's books having to do with animals. He saw *The Rescuers* and *The Wind in the Willows,* as well as a well-thumbed copy of *Black Beauty.* This was Gertie's leisure reading. Something about it touched him: the image of Gertie sitting alone in her dark room, rereading *Black Beauty* for the hundredth time. Gertie had had an inner sensibility, he thought, of which most people were unaware. Who knows what fantasies she had constructed around her life and these books.

"Over here." Snooky was looking at the row of notebooks that marched in hairline precision along the length of a shelf. "Gertie's journals." He took one out at random. The thick looseleaf paper was yellowed with age. "August 4, 1972," he read out loud. "Found an excellent example of the yellow monkey flower *(Mimulus guttatus)* in the woods behind the Folly. Note smooth stem and yellow flowers with closed throats. Sample enclosed." Glued to the page was a brown, dried-out flower. "Saw two raccoons, a hermit thrush and an ovenbird today. Fed the squirrels. There is a family of rabbits in the old burrow near the road. One of them came out and looked at me."

He closed the journal, put it back on the shelf, and drew out another one.

"Found a patch of shinleaf *(Pyrola elliptica)* today. Note greenish-white, waxy flower and reddish stalk."

"Fascinating," said Bernard.

"The most recent one must be at this end," said Snooky. He took it out and thumbed through it. "June . . . July . . . August . . . September . . . nope, this one ends a couple of months ago. 'September 30th—smooth aster *(Aster laevis)*—beautiful sample—note lavender-blue flowers.' That's the last entry. There must be one more journal—the one she was working on when she died."

"Look through her desk."

They moved over to the desk, switched on the green accountant's lamp and began to go through the papers. There were specimens, bits of bark, feathers, leaves, all neatly wrapped in tiny plastic bags and labeled; there were piles of paper with drawings of plants and animals on them in Gertie's tiny, meticulous hand; there was an *Encyclopedia of the Flora and Fauna of the United States,* a thick burgundy-colored book with tissue-thin pages; and there was an assortment of pens, pencils, colored pencils and Magic Markers, all scattered about in confusion. However, there was no journal to be seen. Snooky went through the drawers, one by one. "No. It's not there. Where could she have left it?"

"She was working on it at the time," said Bernard. "Maybe it got reshelved in the wrong place by mistake."

They began to go through the journals one by one,

opening the pages gingerly, glancing through them for dates.

"1971," said Snooky. "1972. 1973."

"1974, 1975, 1976," said Bernard.

"1977, 1978."

"September '79 to November '80."

"December '81 to August '82. Wait a minute." A small yellow piece of paper, folded tightly and wedged between the pages of the journal, had fluttered out when Snooky opened it. "What's this?"

He took it over to the desk and smoothed it out. At the top was printed simply:

MY WILL

I, Gertrude H. Ditmar, do hereby leave all my possessions in the world, including my books, papers, nature journals and whatever share of this house I may own, to the Conservation Society of North America, to be used however they see fit.

It was signed and dated in a flourished script, curiously different from the meticulous writing Gertie used for her scientific observations. It had been witnessed by Irma Ditmar and somebody else whose signature Snooky did not recognize. He glanced up at Bernard. "So now we know how she left it."

"Yes. Keep on looking."

They went through all the journals on the shelf one by one. There were more than forty. At the end, Bernard glanced around the room with a puzzled frown. "Where else could it be?" He moved along the bookcase, running his hand meditatively along the shelves. "Let me see . . . ," he murmured. "Let me see . . . no. Where else? How about . . . *aah!*"

He moved over to the bed, its brass knobs gleaming faintly in the lamplight, and opened the drawer of the rickety wooden bedside table. "Here it is." He took out a large looseleaf notebook. "She must have worked on it in bed before she went to sleep. Let's see now. October fourth . . . October tenth . . . hmmm . . . 'saw a ruffed grouse in the woods on the outskirts of town' . . . hmmm . . . November second . . . here we are. What day was Bobby killed?"

"I don't know. Was it the tenth?"

"Yes. November tenth." Bernard fell silent, absorbed in the pages of the journal.

"Well?" demanded Snooky. "What does it say?"

There was a long silence. Snooky began to feel very cold; a strange creeping kind of coldness, a bitter anticipation. "Well?"

Finally Bernard said slowly, "I don't think we have to worry about any more murders."

"Why? You mean . . . you mean, now that Gertie's dead?"

"No," said Bernard. "I mean now that Irma's dead."

He turned the page around so Snooky could read. There, in Gertie's tiny hand, was the following simple entry:

November 10th—was following a rose-breasted grosbeak with my binoculars in the woods on the edge of town this afternoon when I saw Irma shoot Bobby Fuller in the head. She stood over him for a while, then took the gun and left. It was snowing. I imagine he'll be covered up by now. Good riddance.

And then, at the bottom of the page, almost as an afterthought, Gertie had scrawled,

"I wonder why she did it!"

10

"She did it," said Sarah, "because he told her he was breaking the engagement and leaving her for his girlfriend."

"You knew all along," said Snooky. He and Bernard had come downstairs to find Sarah in the hallway, looking at them in surprise. They had led her into the living room, where Snooky had showed her the journal entry. Sarah read it without emotion.

Now she shook her head. "No. She told me at the end, in the hospital. She knew she was dying. She had one lucid period while I was sitting with her. Can you blame her for wanting to tell somebody? She said she couldn't live with what she had done. That's why she took those pills. She said he was the only man she had ever loved . . . more than she had loved Hugo, even."

Snooky sat her down firmly on a plush green Victorian divan, and drew up a chair next to her. "What did she say?"

Sarah twiddled unhappily with her hair. "It was late one night, in the hospital. She woke up and started to talk. I don't know if she knew it was me sitting there, or a nurse, or Gertie. It didn't seem to matter. She rambled on for over

193

an hour, but what I gathered was that right after they announced their engagement, Bobby told her he was leaving her for this other woman, I don't know her name. Irma took it pretty calmly but arranged to meet him for a final talk the next day, in the woods on the edge of town. She went to Roger's house that morning at a time when she knew he would be out and Dwayne would be downstairs in his darkroom. She knew where the gun was kept, of course. Roger had taught her to handle it years before, and she had picked it up quickly—a little too quickly for his comfort, actually. She took the gun from the closet, loaded it, and left in the car to meet Bobby. I don't know how she explained the gun —I guess she said she was going to try her hand at a little hunting—but they talked it over, and she couldn't convince him to stay with her. He said he was in love with someone else. Well, Irma went a little crazy. She said she felt dizzy and sat down, and when he turned away for a minute, she took the gun and shot him. She stood there for a while over his body, and then left and got in her car and came home. She said she didn't know what happened to the gun; she must have thrown it down on the way to the car. She had been careful to wear gloves when she handled the gun, so there were no fingerprints. With the snow and everything, when the police found the body the next day, there was no evidence that anyone else had been with him."

"And certainly nobody would think of her in connection with his death," said Snooky.

"No. Even though she admitted she had been out that day. She told the police she had gone shopping. And she did do some shopping, on the way home from the woods. She went into Harry's and bought some green beans, and got some chicken from the supermarket and some bread from the bakery. Then she came home and helped me make dinner. She said her mind was working very clearly by then, and she saw how important it was that she act normally. So she and Gertie and I had dinner, and she went to bed early. I never knew a thing."

"And when the news came about Bobby—"

"Well, that's when she had her collapse. Up until then, I think she was denying what she had done. And I don't think she had realized beforehand that the rest of the family would be under suspicion. That's why she held to the idea of a hunting accident. She realized very early on that nobody suspected her, that nobody even knew about the secret girlfriend, that the girlfriend hadn't gone to the police with her story, and that she'd have to do something to protect the rest of us."

"But Gertie knew."

Sarah nodded. "Gertie knew." She motioned toward the journal. "Gertie saw it happen. Gertie and her trusty binoculars."

"Do you think Roger and Dwayne have figured it out?"

"No, I don't think so. I didn't know until Irma told me herself, and it would be impossible for either of them to think that she did it. It was so out of character for her. A crime of passion." Sarah smiled faintly. "You don't think of a woman of nearly seventy as committing a crime of passion, but that's what it was. She said that when Bobby told her he was leaving her, she got so angry that all she wanted to do was kill him."

"And she did."

"Yes. She did." Sarah paused. "After that, she had her good days and her bad days, but she never really got over the shock. Some days she said she could put it out of her mind and think of it as a hunting accident, a terrible tragic accident that could have happened to anybody. But some days she couldn't. And so on one of those days she took an overdose of medication. It was there by her bed, and she said she had been thinking about it for a long time."

Bernard nodded. "The police will have to be told."

"You tell them, then. I'm not having any more to do with that detective."

"Snooky can tell him," said Bernard. "He and Detective Bentley appear to be old friends by now."

"I don't see why I have to do it," said Snooky. "It's not a

pleasant thing talking to Bentley under the best of circumstances. Why can't you tell him?"

"I would, but I can't," said Bernard. "I'm going to be busy."

"Busy? Doing what?"

"Doing something I've looked forward to for a very long time."

Snooky looked at him quizzically. "Really? What's that?"

"Packing to leave."

Snooky dropped Bernard off at the cabin and took the road to Wolfingham. On his way to the police station, he made one short stop. He parked his car on the main street, put his keys in his pocket, and, whistling, walked a few blocks until he found what he was looking for. It was a small store with a red-and-white striped barber pole outside.

He went in and said to the woman behind the counter, "Is Diane here today?"

"Yes. Do you have an appointment?"

"It's not for a haircut. I'd like to talk to her for a moment."

The woman looked him over critically. "You could use a haircut."

"Thank you very much. Another time, perhaps. Is she here?"

"Downstairs."

Snooky went down the steps to a small salon, bright with mirrors, where a gaggle of women were sitting. Diane Caldwell was there, a cigarette in one hand, a cup of coffee in the other.

"You should wear your hair this way, really," she was saying. "Up. It's the newest style. You don't have to cut it, just curl it under like this and fasten it with a—oh!"

"Diane."

She looked frightened. Her lips, Snooky noticed in a detached way, were bright purple today. Her nails were a matching purple and her cheeks were pink. "Yes?"

"Can I talk to you for a second?"

"Sure." She glanced at the women around her. "Ummm . . . upstairs. There's more room upstairs."

They went up to the main floor, their images chasing after them in the mirror-lined walls, and stood near the door, where they could not be overheard. There were several customers in the store, and the room was loud with music, conversation and laughter.

"So then my husband said to me . . ."

"We went to Phoenix last year, what weather, I never in my life . . ."

"I hurt my thumb and I couldn't blow-dry for an entire month. I'm telling you, darling, it was *awful*. My hair looked like a rat's nest . . ."

"Diane."

"Yeah, I'm listening. What is it?"

He told her.

She listened to his story in silence. At the end, she stubbed out her cigarette in a nearby ashtray. "I see."

"He was going to leave her for you."

"Uh-huh."

They were silent. Around them swirled the unrelated conversations of other lives. Diane appeared to be deep in thought, her magenta lips pursed together.

"He loved me best, the bastard."

Snooky nodded.

"I told you he loved me best."

"Yes. You did."

"Thank you for coming."

They shook hands, and she went back downstairs. The woman behind the counter said something as she passed. Diane threw back her head and, with a return of her old spirit, said, "None of your beeswax, Charlene!"

———

197

Bernard packed his suitcases with a great sense of joy and relief. He trundled them out to the car and stood waiting, shivering in the cold, for Maya. During the past few days Snooky had outdone himself as a host. One excellent gustatory experience had followed another, until now, at last, it was time to leave. Even Maya agreed that they had been away too long.

"You're right, sweetheart," she had said the night before, in bed. "Now that I know Snooky's safe, I can leave."

"Snooky's always safe. The shadow of death passes over his head."

"I certainly hope so. Why are you so grouchy?"

Bernard moved restlessly under the covers. "Misty's taking up too much room under here. I don't care if she is cold, I'm tired of having her in bed with us."

"Put her out, then. She can sleep near the fire."

Misty looked at him in horrified reproach as he dumped her over the side. She resignedly padded off to sleep, as Maya had predicted, near the warm embers of the hearth. "That's better."

"Why, look, darling, we're alone," said Maya, and edged closer to him. Bernard felt his contentment grow and expand in a joyful bubble as he gathered her into his arms.

Now he stood shivering as Maya and Snooky came out of the cabin arm in arm. They were laughing, heads thrown back, the same laugh, the same pose. Like twins, Bernard reflected sourly. The good twin and her evil twin. Snooky was carrying Misty in his other arm. He dumped her in the back seat of the car, where she sat drooling with anticipatory nausea at the trip.

"There she is. She looks a little green already, Bernard. If I were you, I'd drive fast, or stop often, or both. She doesn't look to me like she's going to make it."

"Misty hates to travel."

"Like her owner."

"Yes."

"Well, thank you for coming. May I say it's been wonderful working my fingers to the bone for the two of you. You are the perfect guests—almost as perfect as I am."

"We're not in your league, Snooks," said Maya, giving him a motherly peck on the cheek. "But then, of course, we haven't had the kind of practice you have."

"Take care of yourselves. Have a safe trip home."

Bernard opened the door for Maya, then went around and got in the driver's seat. "Just one thing, Snooky," he said, leaning out the window.

"Yes?"

"Try to give us a running start before you get in your car and come visit us, all right?"

"I'm sorry to disappoint you, but I already have other plans. Sarah and I are heading north in a week or so. I have friends in Canada, you know."

This came as no surprise. Snooky had a seemingly infinite network of friends spread out over the continental United States, Canada and Mexico, all of whom appeared to be delighted to see him on a moment's notice.

Maya lifted an eyebrow. "You and Sarah?"

"Yes. She's forgiven me for searching through Gertie's belongings. And the Wuxlers are coming back soon to claim their cabin."

"Have a good time," said Bernard, withdrawing his head like a turtle into the recesses of the car.

"Thanks. I will."

"Don't go looking for trouble."

"I never go looking for it, Bernard. It seems to come and find me. Have a good trip."

"So long."

"So long!" called Maya. She waved at her brother as the car moved off gingerly down the bumpy road, and Misty prepared herself to be sick in the back seat.

Bernard sat, contented as a king, enthroned in the red leather chair in his study. There was a cup of coffee steaming on his desk, Misty was snoring at his feet, and there was a light snow falling outside. The blue light slanting in

199

through the narrow windows was, Bernard felt, the perfect touch to a perfect scene. He and Maya had arrived home several weeks ago to find that the house had not been burglarized and stripped of its contents, that old Mr. Sanders from next door had hobbled across their adjoining lawns like clockwork, once a week, to take care of the plants in the solarium and collect the mail, and that life in Ridgewood, Connecticut, was in fact as perfect as Bernard remembered it. Maya had looked over the jungle of plants in the sun room with a faintly disappointed air.

"What's the matter?"

"It's these plants."

Bernard looked around. The plants looked wonderful; if anything, larger, glossier and healthier than before they went away. "What? They look fine."

"That's the problem, Bernard. They look more than fine. They look terrific. They look better than when I take care of them."

"Mr. Sanders used to be a gardener."

"Mr. Sanders knows something I don't."

"You could ask him."

Maya sniffed and turned away, twiddling disconsolately with the end of a vine.

Now Bernard sat at his typewriter, looking at a page of the Mrs. Woolly manuscript. It was the final scene, and Mrs. Woolly was lecturing the children on the lessons they had learned. Mrs. Woolly's great-nephew, Kiddykins, was cavorting on a slope nearby, and at the end the children went and played with him. The sun was a large bright disk in the sky, and it was hot where Mrs. Woolly was, in the middle of the endless summer of Woolly-land. Bernard grunted and ran a finger around his shirt collar. It was hot where he was, too. The rickety old Victorian where he and Maya lived was riddled with cracks where the wind blew in, so he had lugged an old space heater into his study, which was now filling the room with stifling heat. Bernard switched it off. Poor Misty, he thought. She must be nearly cooked by now.

2 0 0

He got up slowly, lost in a dream of Woolly-land, and opened the window a few inches, enough to let the chill air in. He stood at the window for a moment, meditating, and as he stood there he became faintly aware of a ringing sound. His study door was closed, but it seemed to him . . . yes, it must be the telephone . . .

He opened the door and stood listening. Yes. The telephone in the master bedroom. He scowled. Maya was out for the afternoon and she had asked him to answer the phone and take a message. Of course it would not be for him; it so rarely was. Only Maya had friends who bothered to telephone. Occasionally Bernard's agent or publisher called, but that was all, and he had spoken to both of them only the day before.

He went into the bedroom, sat down heavily on the edge of the great bed with its carved oak frame, and regarded the ringing telephone with a solemn expression in his eyes. Perhaps if he didn't answer it . . . perhaps if he moved his hand so very slowly that he couldn't get to it in time . . . perhaps then it would stop ringing and whoever was on the other end would go away, or call again at a better time, when Maya was in. Perhaps if he moved his hand ever so slowly . . .

He counted nine, ten, eleven rings. At last, with a sigh, he picked up the receiver. "Hello?"

"I knew you were there," said Snooky. He sounded far away, disembodied, like a voice from Mars.

"Good Lord. Where are you calling from?"

"Banff, Canada."

"Oh."

"If you're answering the phone, Bernard, I assume that my sister isn't home, or that you have her bound and gagged in the closet."

"That's right."

"So I'll talk to you." Snooky's voice sounded so far away it was practically ethereal; Bernard felt he was hearing the voice of an angel, except for the occasional spurt of static across the line.

"What's going on? How's Sarah?"

"She's fine."

"Say hello from us."

"I will."

There was a long silence, interspersed with the cheerful crackle of static.

"Thank you for calling," said Bernard. "I have to go now."

"You're sure my sister isn't home?"

"Quite sure."

"Oh. Well, listen. I'd rather have suggested this to her, but . . . I'm calling to ask if the two of you would like to come up here sometime. It's even more beautiful than the cabin—we've rented this Swiss chalet-type thing—and there's more than enough room. Sarah and I would love it if the two of you could visit."

"No, thank you."

"It wouldn't have to be right away. I know how you feel about traveling. But I think you'd be missing something if you didn't come, Bernard. It's breathtakingly beautiful here. The mountains are incredible, and there's great skiing—oh, you don't ski, do you?"

"No."

"Well, you could learn. I know Maya loves to ski. I don't ski much myself, but Sarah goes on the slopes and I sit by the fire. There's a beautiful indoor swimming pool here, with glass walls all around. And there are caribou, Bernard."

"Caribou?"

"Herds of them. They roam across the fields at dusk. The most gorgeous creatures you've ever seen. Caribou, or maybe elk. Sarah says they're elk, but I'm not sure. Can you tell the difference?"

"No."

"Neither can I. Gertie would have known. But they're something, all right. You've never seen anything like it. The mountains go as far as the eye can see. And it's been snowing here, Bernard—*real* snow—about three feet of it. It's a winter paradise. The chalet is very comfortable, and there's plenty of room for everybody. You could fly out of New York and be here in the morning."

"What's the temperature?"

"The temperature? Oh, I don't know. About fifteen below, I think. Of course, at night it's much colder."

"Good-bye, Snooky. Thank you for calling."

"Don't go yet, Bernard. Wait a minute. Perhaps I haven't described it fully enough. The mountains go as far as the eye can see. Did I say that already? They're spectacular. And the caribou or elk or whatever they are run across our lawn at night. You could sit and have hot chocolate by the fire, and in the evenings I would cook for you. Beef stew, Bernard. Beef stew every night. And the stars. Did I mention them already? The stars are incredible. Sarah and I go outside and look at them for hours. You can see the Milky Way. The stars look like—like jewels across the sky."

"Good-bye."

"Wait. Do me one favor before you go. Please tell Maya I called. I know there's only a fifty-fifty chance you will, but I'd like to speak to her. Here's my number. Do you have a pencil and paper?"

"Yes," said Bernard, who didn't.

"Good. Here's my number. Six oh four—that's the area code—six oh four, five nine two—"

"What?"

"Six oh four, that's the area code, five nine two—"

"What?"

"SIX OH FOUR, THAT'S THE AREA CODE, FIVE NINE TWO . . ."

Bernard tapped the receiver impatiently. "I can't hear you, Snooky. It's all static on my side. Would you try that number again? Say it louder this time."

"SIX OH FOUR," shrieked Snooky's voice across the miles and miles of snow and wilderness separating Banff, Canada, from the milder plains of Ridgewood, Connecticut. "SIX OH FOUR, FIVE NINE TWO . . ."

"I'm losing the connection," bellowed Bernard. He

tapped at it again. "Can you hear me? It's just static, Snooky. Can you hear me? I can't hear anything at all. You're fading."

"SIX OH FOUR," shrieked the voice from the northern wilderness, in a tone of mingled rage and despair. "FIVE NINE TWO . . ."

"I have to go now, Snooky. I'm so sorry. I can't hear you at all. It's a long way, you know. A long way for a person to travel. I hope you can hear me, because I've lost you completely. Good-bye. Thanks again for calling."

"BERNARD," came a wail from the other end of the phone. Bernard winced and held the phone away from his ear.

"I'M SORRY," he bawled into the receiver. "I CAN'T HEAR YOU, SNOOKY. GOOD-BYE. CALL AGAIN ANOTHER TIME."

"BERNARD," cried the voice in a shrill wail. "PLEASE TELL MAYA I SAID . . ."

"Good-bye," said Bernard, and replaced the receiver gently on its hook.

147738

DATE DUE
